I0544268

Live Free

A novel by Caroline Durand

First Edition
978-0-578-61683-4

ii

For Emily and Dominic
And for Robert

Contents

Part I Slavery 2

    Honor Among Thieves.............................2

    In the Rough.......................................7

    Eye of the Beholder............................21

    War and Peace....................................27

    Vengeance 32

    Flight from Egypt................................44

    Terra Incognita 50

    NewIstanbul 66

Part II Second Comings 71

    Erroneous Reasoning 71

    Out of the Frying Pan.........................78

    Into the Fire 85

    Improv 93

    Hamartia of the Heart.......................101

    Discoveries..104

Part III War at Home 109

    Unbroken..109

    What NewAmerica Holds 114

    Reality Check.....................................122

    Mouth of the Beast...........................126

    Janus...132

    Hide and Seek 141

Part IV Death, Us Part 147

    Shut Down..147

    Out of Darkness................................154

    Undone 162

    Paris Once More...............................170

    The Truth..174

    Epilogue 177

Amity Agreement

The world will be split into four zones, keeping the creeds separate. The first, the Believers of Love, will inhabit NewAmerica. The second, the Believers of Power, will be confined to the continent of the United Sahara. The third, the Believers of Serenity, will dwell in Serens, formally known as Asia and Australia. Finally, The Free Zone, once Europe, will remain unaffiliated, a haven for those who believe in no creed.

This action, taken by the World Authority Association, shall be implemented to ensure that the three creeds will be unable to interact without express permission from the Association. The members of these creeds will also be treated as locked-zone citizens, contained in their own quadrant, given redded travel passports, marked as politically unengaged civilians, and will be exempt from laws concerning natural rights. With no interaction and no power, they will not begin another nuclear engagement, and humanity will be forevermore safe from the destruction that was the Credo Wars.

Part I Slavery

Honor Among Thieves

I drew the knife along the curved wall of the sewers, watching as the mucky algae collected on the sharp edge. The lethal silver and the dirty green made for an interesting clash of color. I enjoyed the line of destruction it created as it dragged along.

Taking in his grimy figure, I paused for only a moment, the walls tainted yellow by the lighting of the poor illumination sensors. The smell was horrid enough to gag. Which he did.

Face scrunched against the smell, he held his hand to his nose. He'd been standing still for some time, his torn jacket slick against his shirt, waiting for me to acknowledge him.

My silver boots sunk in the muck as my eyes flashed. "Paris," I scoffed. My voice echoed, mixing with the water dripping from the walls. Like many others in the NewAmerican area, his name was a testament to the world before the Credo Wars. Paris. A city from long ago.

"Shandra, my darling." His casual use of such an endearment made me pause for a moment, but he wasn't worth my rage. "I hear you're looking for information," he rasped. "I presume you can pay." He ran a hand across his brow.

"Only if you can deliver." He wasn't the first bounty hunter I'd hired, and they hadn't found leads worth paying for.

"Oh, I assure you, I'm not like the rest. And neither, I've heard, are you. Unless MiraCorp has fallen on bad times? Has the Green Tree of Medicine lost its value? There hasn't been much war of late, and I do know how that drives up business."

I ignored his jibe. I was Shandra Lux. The fact he knew this made little difference. "I have questions."

"Ask away, then." His teeth shining, he pressed his fingertips together.

Information was what this pathetic maggot traded. He would receive a payment, but he would know what was driving me, what I wanted. That data was something he could send to others, to warn them of my coming.

No. That could not happen. I would ask him. If he didn't intend to keep secrets, I didn't intend to keep my hands clean. "I'm looking for someone."

His greedy fingers thrummed against his leg. "Indeed?"

His seconds were crawling away, so I spoke the truth. "Her name is Nessa—Vanessa."

He snorted, his lips twisting upward. "Nessa. NewAmerican for *pure*. A name of Credo origin. A Believer? I didn't take you as the sort to dabble in the ways of the weak."

I snarled, baring my teeth. "I don't believe in anything. Those fools destroyed my world over their pointless views." Their war got my parents killed. I folded my arms. I had more right to blame the Believers than others did, but Nessa was different. "I just want to find her."

"To kill her?" he offered, intrigued by my interest in such a lowly citizen. Even in NewAmerica, a Believer could be murdered in broad daylight, and it was practically endorsed by the World Authority Association. The unaffiliated would simply walk over the cold carcasses.

But not Nessa. A memory of her, standing in a political crowd, flashed. She came beside me, the only person in the room who wasn't a liar and a sophist. The sound of her laughter bouncing around the reception room drew many handsome eyes to her, but she ignored them, continuing her saga to me, the latest gossip she needed to catch me up on. Her story inevitably ended with her belief that my own heartlessness was just an act, that I wasn't what was wrong with the world. How blind she'd been. How refreshing, innocently, hopelessly blind.

"Ah." He grinned. "Someone you would pay much for. This truly could be a ransom."

"This is not a kidnapping." I put my hands into the pockets of my long black jacket. "I would have paid the bribe, but no note came."

He wheezed. "I'm sure. Do you have a description of her I can work with?" He asked his question with a calculating look, focused on the task before him.

"She's smaller, a petite person with brown hair. She's a Believer. She's probably broke. And… she's got brown eyes." Were her eyes brown?

"Where did you see her last?"

"During the spring, half a year ago. She took an illegal trip to the Believer holy place, Garheen."

"Those trips are not as uncommon as you might think. The World Authority Association found there's a high rate of terminal interactions in the city. Now, they turn a blind eye, let the Believers leave, and hope they die." He pressed his lips together. "What flight number?"

Gritting my teeth, my hands formed into fists. I was an idiot for not keeping tabs on her. I let her leave the country, and I never bothered to make sure she came back. "Flight 472." I paused. "You think that's what happened?"

"Ah. 472." His fingers twitching, he smirked. "I hear that a transport of religious pilgrims was shot down outside the castle of the Brokel Stroben, of the Burning Tree. She, the Brokel, likes to prey on the religious travelers, what with their undercover nature. She collects them, and they rot in her palace, on the edge of the desert in the United Sahara. If there are survivors left, they could be with her."

"Walk into a Brokel's castle?" He must have thought I had a death wish. "Good plan."

His tongue flickered. "You just need the right materials. The government of the NewAmerican Alliance executed Luna Storm. She was a bounty hunter, paid by Stroben to kill a gang leader over here. Stroben knows she finished her job, but the Brokel doesn't know she was killed. Few know that."

I began to understand what he was suggesting. "I masquerade as this woman to gain entrance to the palace, and I find the truth for myself." I wasn't sold just yet.

His reptilian features bobbed in a nod. "You have no religious affiliation, so you can travel whenever you want. Stroben usually doesn't meet her hitmen until after they've completed their kill. She's never seen Storm. She wouldn't know the difference between you and her. I have the bounty hunter's signature armor with me, in a safe place. It will cost a small fortune, but you're Shandra Lux, the great owner of the Green Tree of MiraCorp. I'm sure you'll pay."

I laughed. I could pay any data-miner in the city, and they'd create a copy of the outfit. I didn't need to buy anything from Paris. In fact, with his loose lips, I only had one more order of business.

At least I didn't need to make this neat, and I didn't need to terminate him. A bit of threatening and some pain would convince him to keep his mouth shut.

After all, in this grime, a bit of blood on my jacket would be nothing.

In the Rough

I was standing in the sick heat at the edge of this desert hodgepodge, already sweating. Traveling over had given me the time to put together a replica of Storm's armor and study her habits. When I first arrived, I bought a TerrieV 29 transport rover, for the sake of my escape, if need be. I had it parked near the food preparation entrance, off in a forgotten portion of the castle. But I wasn't about to sneak around, not when I was in the guise of a bounty hunter. As Luna Storm, I would walk right in. And so, I stood, staring at the fortress, at its black monolithic structure, with two towers spiraling out above it.

But between me and the entrance, there was a town, a moldlike growth. The city, if it could be called as much, was expansive, each wall caked with dust that had been born of sand. Each corner, each doorway, each hovel, was accented by this silt. The vehicles, the buildings, the people, were drowned by the tan of the grit and the black of the palace.

Coming towards me, out of the city, was the caretaker of the Palace Stroben. "Right this way." He gestured forward, through a bleached pathway. "I trust you will find your accommodations quite comfortable. I saw to it myself. It's designed for a traveler from the NewAmericas." He smoothed out his black tunic, adorned with the red crest of

Stroben, a burning tree. "It even has a cooling unit, and entertainment technology, Hunter Storm."

I grunted in a half second of surprise at being called Storm, not Shandra, but I covered it with a shrug. "I could care less for your frivolities," I almost didn't get the words out. "I wish to meet with Stroben to speak of payment." I needed to find out about the passengers from Flight 472.

"It may take some time to set up a meeting, as they are celebrating a victory. One of Stroben's rivals, a Brokel from the south, has fallen from power." He paused for a long moment. "Although, perhaps I could be persuaded to meditate on her schedule further."

I drew out the Universal Currency, the UVs, passing over a twenty. It was a price high enough to incentivize him, but little more.

He grinned as we reached the palace entrance. "As is the custom, she will discuss payment over a victory dinner, to thank you during the financing. This afternoon, Stroben will be executing the family of a rival Brokel. The dinner will be served after the celebration."

I see," I said dryly.

"And of course, you'll want to know what we have to offer while you are here. There are four expansive levels at the Castle. Your quarters are here on the second floor, along with the other guests' rooms. The floor also features a security room, training areas, and Stroben's quarters, none of which permit visitors. Above us, there is the observation area, where you can view the garden, watch the caging of low security prisoners, and look down upon the surrounding town. Below us, on the first floor, there is the throne-room and the meeting area. If you're interested, there is a trophy room, too. The staff and slave areas are in the basement."

How could he talk this much?

He continued, oblivious. "Though it may also be worth your time, Hunter Storm, to join in the festivities this afternoon. It is worth reveling in the death of anyone the Brokel deems unworthy."

I drew closer, hiding my annoyance under a mask of serenity. This rambler likely had an allegiance to money, more than he did to the Brokel. "Noted. One more thing. The passengers from Flight 472. There are whispers that Stroben had them shot down. What do you think happened?"

"It is not my place to say." His shoulders lifted in an impression of false innocence.

"Come now. You're the caretaker of the palace, you hear things. Tell me." I drew out more UVs.

"They crashed. Officially, no survivors. But it was obvious where her new batch of humans came from. They were brought in."

Nessa was on that plane. So, she crashed. She could be alive.

"Can you find out where the survivors are?" I reached, while I asked, into my pocket, pulling out five hundred UVs. "I'd make it worth your time. Half now, and half when you return."

The servant reached out his hand, accepting the cash. "I can," he offered, took the money, and turned on his heel.

Left in the silence, I stared at the synthetic adobe walls that surrounded me, at the crests that were the signature of the Brokel. Nessa had probably seen that same symbol. I could picture it, her wide eyes and innocent expression as she stared at the burning branches. But then, her face always looked surprised by the world around her, even when we first met.

I saw her at this celebration of a World Authority Politician. I'd only been invited because of my wealth. Granted, this time, it was a celebration for the first Believer to be voted in, so the people who came were not the normal crowd, not that I fit in with any crowd. True to who I was, I stood on the outskirts, bored and above this, watching as couples kissed and groups laughed. But for the first time, someone stepped out of the horde and spoke to me.

She began by telling stories about her most recent break-up, while also asking who I was, what I was like, lamenting that I had no boyfriend of my own. Men kept interrupting us, asking this charismatic woman to dance, but she turned them down, informing them of her serious conversation. I told her she was missing her chance to find a new man, but she only laughed, telling me she would only marry a man who brought her flowers. None of them did.

By the end of the night, she informed me that I'd passed her test, that we were friends. Our strange bond continued, the depth of our conversations moving from boyfriends to philosophy, to war relief efforts, back to boyfriends, while her charisma and energy remained a constant. I didn't even know she was a Believer until I went to her apartment for the first time, a place in the slums.

I offered to buy her a new house, a mansion if she wanted it, but she was intent on building her way up on her own. She was painstakingly putting away every penny to remodel. The hard work was a virtue in her Believer mindset.

Despite this ideal, one or two of her many bills would be paid mysteriously. After all, if she lost her apartment, the only place we could hang out was my place, and mine was boring. It was the least I could do for the only friend I really had, the only person who believed in me. She always said I was a good person, someone who could inspire others, change the world. It was the only topic on which we disagreed. I was selfish, moody, angry. I was nothing like a hero.

I glanced at the sharp, expensive furnishings around me, at the burning tree symbol. Did being here prove me right, or her? And did one small act of good change who I was? I snorted, thinking of my dealings with Paris. I was not good.

But now was not the time to dwell on my inner self. I was in the lair of the warlord. I had to find Nessa. I needed any clues this palace gave me. This celebration was a perfect place to begin my search. As I moved through the building to the festivities room, a bead of sweat dripped down my neck. Would Nessa be here?

I stepped into the gathering, hearing the overwhelming music of a low bass blare into my ears. Through a haze of smoke, on the sides of the room, there were tables heaped with foods from every part of the world. A man I slid by grabbed for a coconut slice from the Serens, and a woman who stumbled into me smelled of lamb from the unaffiliated lands. As I passed by bodyguards and bounty hunters, there was cheese from NewAmerica and hummus from the Believers of Power. There were even uncooked delicacies from the Believers of Serenity. As I stepped through the group, I caught sight of the center of the room, the throne. My eyes widened at the sight of the golden chair, placed on a platform surrounded by food and drinks and servants.

There, in a chair of brown oak melting into flame, was Brokel Stroben. The light reflecting off her bald forehead, she watched a broad-shouldered pet of hers, a man my age. This servant was wearing the crest of the Castle Stroben, painted on his chest, a stark contrast to Stroben's black tunic. She leaned in, speaking inaudibly to him.

In response to her words, the toned man turned away, toward me. His face was marked by woven strips, tattoos running from one ear to the other, passing over his nose, marking him as a slave. His face flushed deeply, accenting his sharp jaw, but he stooped low, picking up a pitcher, pouring wine into his master's waiting goblet. I stared at him as he knelt once more, wondering if he was a reflection of Nessa. My chest suddenly hurt.

As she leaned forward, the muscles on Stroben's sleeveless arm budged. She glanced around the room with a look of disinterest. But in a flutter, her face contorted. She made a gesture, and a commotion exploded from the far side of the room.

A security man shoved a prisoner forward, the convict stumbling as they moved. He was led to the center of the room while onlookers stared in sudden silence. I watched with mild interest, taking in this man, his strong frame accented by threadbare clothing.

Stroben leaned forward. "Jooka, you are the only brother of Brokel Noon. As such, you are the sole heir to the blood right. For this, I sentence you to exile. You will be brought to NewAmerica and sold as chattel. Your lands, your peoples, and your world will be annexed into my empire."

The man's eyes snapped up. "Your methods lack honor. The other Brokels will hear of this. As will the world."

"Perhaps." She waved a hand carelessly. "But not from you. Now. Why not a punishing, first?"

"A warrior does not cower under such words." He spat at the ground. "Do your work, and do it quickly." He stared forward, no longer acknowledging the Brokel.

"Perhaps a whipping." She glanced to her slave, her fingers reaching out. In a moment, they laced themselves through his hair, and I winced. "But the cries of torment do upset my Favored One so, don't they?"

Her coy tone was cutting into my temperate mask. It took a moment to recenter myself, to remind myself that I was Shandra, that I cared for nothing and no one but Nessa, that I was without feeling.

The slave with the pitcher cleared his throat. "Your judgements are wise and final, Master."

"And I have chosen for you to determine his punishment. Tell us, Favored One, how should I chastise him for his insults?"

The Favored One opened his mouth to speak, but no words spilled out. He simply looked at the condemned man as Jooka stared back. The slave's throat worked, his tongue twitching between his perfect teeth, but the silence was only broken by the quiet laughter of onlookers.

"Imprisonment?" Stroben offered.

The slave's hazel eyes focused on the liquid he was holding.

"Electrocution, then?"

His perfectly manicured face paled, even as he attempted a look of blankness.

"Poison? Ah, but then we'd have to be careful not to kill him."

He flinched.

"Let this man be brought a goblet of hemlock, to be drank until empty." The Favored One finally looked to Stroben, defeated. "And do not give the antidote until my slave sees fit."

The crowd, hearing the finality in her voice, roared with approval. But as for me, I saw enough. I knew now that Stroben grew her power from a place of power and violence. She took her title as Brokel to heart. She lived by the way of the warlords.

The slave turned his face away from his master, his eyes a glassy and glazed mix of green and brown. Slightly hidden from her, he gave a tormented exhale, his jaw locked with profound frustration. Before him, there were the broken shards from the pitcher he'd been holding. I'd missed when he dropped it.

My own hands were bunched into fists. I relaxed them, shaking my shoulders out as I turned away, leaving the celebration.

I stepped through the hallways, pacing silently past rich decorations and expensive artworks. My reality was that I had to have a cool head before the upcoming dinner, and I was not currently tranquil. It was as simple as that, and nothing more. I continued pacing, meditating on the upcoming event, as the minutes turned to hours, afternoon to night.

As dusk settled over the sands, I strode back towards the main area of the palace. I came to the dining chambers, ready to discuss financing, still garbed in the red armor of my faux persona. The metal of the armor was glinting in the poor lighting, the deep red cloth underneath projecting a threatening aura. Even the hard tapping of my boots against the marble floor was empowering.

The Brokel, having taken note of my entrance, pointed to a place at the feast. As I took in the two bodyguards behind her, she flashed a smile that I knew wouldn't last. "Storm."

Even now, sitting before the Brokel, I had difficulty accepting this fake name, still expecting the sound of *Shandra*. But this time, I was able to take it without reaction. I went to my place, noting the subtle lift of the table. There were three sections, each of a different height, like petals on a stem. The highest, hers, was accented by golden plates and the finest of salted meats, perfect fruits. At my place, lower on this table, the meat was slightly overcooked, the dishware silver. But it was a feast when compared to the third placement, so lowered that the occupant would have to sit on the floor.

Seeing me glance to this third location, the Brokel Stroben lifted a brow, gesturing to it. "For my Favored One." She waved a hand.

One disdainful bodyguard, a woman with weapons lining her torso, knives decorating her jacket, rods and guns across her belt, her nails filed to sharp points, reached behind the throne, grabbing for something. She reappeared, holding the arm of the slave I saw at the celebration. With a loathing shove, she sent the pet to the ground.

The slave crawled over to the place. Even in this darkened, smoky room, his hazel eyes were brought out by the tattoo strip across his face. His broad shoulders came to rest as his fingers twitched, aware of so much food within reach. But he ironed the desperation away from his eyes, into the muscles of his neck, the tightening of his jaw, the slight bend of his lips. Nessa used to make the same expression.

In the silence, I watched one of the male bodyguards step forward once more. Seemingly unarmed, he began tasting a small portion of each delicacy before the Brokel. After a silent moment, this dangerous minion stepped back in a sneering gesture, crossing his unequipped arms. As he stepped beside the lethal woman, the meal began. A taste tester.

I tilted my jaw to Stroben. "Worried I might taint your food?"

Biting into a hybridgo, she lifted an eyebrow. "Hardly. It's not you." She gestured to her chattel meaningfully. "But my Favored One has learned his place, hasn't he?"

The young man shifted, his shaven face blushing. He bowed his head further down, as if he wanted to bring himself so far that he'd simply slip through the floor.

Had he poisoned her? I blinked at his toned torso. He must have been—

"Ah, yes. He came to me with far too much insurgence. At the beginning, he attempted to fight my decisions. He actually thought his pleas would save the lives of the condemned." Stroben directed little of her attention to me. This discussion was for the benefit, or the shaming, of the slave. "He took a great deal of time adjusting to his status as my personal Favored One. And then, right when I thought I'd tamed him, he tried to poison me."

His neck flushed, but he allowed no movement to indicate he had even heard her.

"What he didn't realize was that my slaves are injected with a tracker. It's like a leash, so my property doesn't stray. Favored One, show her where your tracker is."

Robotically, he lifted his arm onto the table, palm up, as he pointed to a location mere inches below his hand, next to his cuffs. "It's here," he said blankly, his monotone voice contrasting with his flushed face. "Next to my vein." Though I'd thrown up a wall to keep my emotions hidden, I still felt a strike of pain for this man, for his evident misery.

"I knew he'd attended a gathering of rebels. With him dining at my feet, poison seemed to be the obvious choice." She laughed. "I killed the others. But my Favored One? I punished him well enough."

The man blinked rapidly as he stared at his wrist.

"What can I say? I like them with fight in them, and this one's a little devil." She snapped her fingers, a signal to the slave to look up. "Aren't you?"

His first reaction was to flinch, drawing his hand back in a protective gesture. Then, surprised, he cleared his throat. "Yes, master." His tone was a soft murmur. "A devil, master. But I've learned my place."

Stroben and I moved to haggling on my payment. The disagreement was a simple discussion for me to navigate. I was Shandra Lux, and I owned a company. And while I was not wholly committed to it, I did my fair share of negotiations. This discussion, like them, was easy.

We agreed on a fair price for Luna's kill and I stood to leave, finished with bartering over the cost of a murder. As I got up, the Favored One rose as well. It was the custom here, a formality I cared little for, for the slave to stand as I left. But in his action, he fumbled, catching himself on the table. It was a movement made sloppy by his decorative cuffs, and he almost knocked away the small bread bowl in front of him.

Righting himself, he went rigid. A small grunt escaped his lips, but nothing more happened.

I stared at this man. He had been graceful before. Now he was suddenly clumsy? Unless— I looked down at the setting that was before him, realizing that the amount of food had lessened.

He had stolen from the table and had tried to hide the action from his master. A small smile crept up my lips as I flickered my attention back to the Brokel. She, too, wore a slight, if disturbed, grin.

I wondered if this handsome man thought he was fooling anyone. Or was he just hoping no one would address his actions? He looked to me quickly, reading in my features the futility of his charade.

Then he glanced to his owner, breaking the rule of unrequested eye-contact. She only stared back, now unreadable. The slave could not tell if his master knew. And the Brokel wanted it that way. Not a word was said about the theft as I left the room.

Eye of the Beholder

I stood outside the reception room for some time after I left. After so much waiting, my shoes sunk into the rich rug from the Islands. Bored, I stared at the same ugly painting from the Old Americas. Each object, each accent within sight was a reminder of who had authority, and who did not.

It was intended to be belittling, but my wealth was a power of its own. While I feigned attention to the aesthetics, I was waiting for the servant to exit.

When the slave finally stepped into the hallway, my focus instantly fell upon him. The door closed behind him and he leaned against it, thinking himself finally alone. Bringing the back of his palm to his face, he rubbed his hand over the markings on his face. Lethargically, he let his hands fall back to his side. He looked exhausted, and I hurt for him, even if only for a moment. But then the second passed, and I refocused. Nessa was all I cared about.

I observed dispassionately as he gave a sigh and made his way down the corridors, turning away from me. He found his way down a stairwell to a servant level, bare feet hushed as he walked. I followed, my strides silent.

When two bounty hunters, half-way down the steps, sneered at him, he shivered. After a short second, he crossed his arms and they baited him, aware of his social inability to fight back. He hurried past. The idiots didn't even notice moments later as I swiftly passed by in the shadows.

The slave made his way to the servant's corridor, near where he must live. In these hallways, the walls were brown, windowless, depressing. It was an area to store the slaves, a packing location, not a display area.

As the man walked in the shadows, he paused, glancing over his shoulder. Had anyone else been in the hallway, he would have seen them and fled. But I embraced the darkness, mixing with the shadows, and his gaze passed over me, unable to distinguish nightmare from reality.

Then he slipped into the residence of the other slaves, the lowest class. Staring at where he was, I blinked, not bothering to hide my surprise. This man was a Favored One. He was supposed to be kept separate. If Stroben knew that her precious puppet was doing this, socializing with the lowest of the low—He had to have a death wish.

But for a person of a high class to step into those quarters, someone like me? A hitman who had honored the Brokel with her kill? I could go wherever I wanted. I went inside.

"Where is he?" I demanded of the first slave I saw.

The girl's face whitened as her eyes widened. With a terrified flicker of her hand, she pointed down to the end of the hall. In the underlit, filthy corridor, there was a tucked away corner. I stepped over, passing by small hovels, rooming areas with small groups and families of slaves, all recoiling as I passed.

After a bend in the hallway, the path abruptly ended, opening to three figures in the corner. He was one of them.

I stared at him, interested in what in here was worth dying for. He was turned away from the entrance, his back still unrobed, the muscles flexing with his movements as he crouched. In a hushed tone, he was speaking with an ill woman while another lady stood, overlooking their interaction.

"This is what we've got for now, Irene." He was holding out the small loaf from dinner. "But I'll be back with more later."

The sick woman, laying in the corner, moved, attempting to sit. The Favored One gripped her arm, helping her lean into the dark wall in the corner. "Careful. You need to save your strength. You can sit up again when you get better."

The slave coughed. "They say I'm not going to get better." Her small voice was almost too quiet to hear.

He shook his head, his shoulders straightening as he leaned back. "Who says that? I hope you told them how wrong they were."

"Were they?" Her voice shook.

"They were." He reached out, grabbing her hand for a long moment. "Your job right now is to sleep and heal. I'll take care of everything else." After a moment, still turned away from me, he got to his feet.

The standing woman shook her head, her simple white tunic shifting with her movement. "There's no hope for her, not if we can't get a doctor to look at her, give her meds." She was whispering, trying not to let Irene overhear. "She's running out of time. Can you speak to the master again?"

The man nodded his head. "Of course. Don't give up hope, Virginia."

The woman, Virginia, apparently, touched her hand to her forehead. "I only wish there was another way. Irene doesn't have much time left. She's too sick to serve. If she doesn't serve, they don't feed her. If she isn't fed, she won't heal." Tears tore their way into her voice. "Please save her."

"I'll come back tomorrow with more food. Was York able to stop by with the herbs?" He rubbed the back of his neck in a slow motion.

"He came, but he wasn't able to steal them." She sniffed. "He's worried Koren is on to him."

The slave, still shrouded in shadows, gave a long sigh. "Then we'll come up with another way. Do what you can for her. I'll think of something."

The Favored One glanced to the ailing girl one final time and turned to leave. Now out of the view of both slaves, his face was suddenly strained, his eyebrows pressed down. I wondered just how many ideas he had left.

As he stepped out, his eyes found their way to me. I started, but his face whitened, reminding me that I had caught him in an illegal act, not the other

24

way around. He paused in the doorway between the room and the hallway. Here was a slave who dared to steal from the Brokel, only to break into a place where he was not allowed, to feed a slave the masters had deemed unworthy.

His expression faltered, flashing panic, as he realized just how much illicit activity I'd seen. He hissed out in a fast breath. "Are you going to tell?" He was suddenly profoundly interested in the grey tiles on the ground and the small hovels behind me. After a heartbeat of silence, he wrapped his arms around his chest, covering Stroben's brand.

"Perhaps." Would I tell anyone about his deeds? No. But he didn't need to know that.

He swallowed hard, slipping past me. As he walked down the hallway, he seemed to shrink, as if maybe if he tried harder, he could turn invisible, and no longer be a part of this horrible world.

I looked to the sickly slave woman. The healthy one knelt beside her, oblivious to my presence. Wiping tears from her eyes, she gripped her friend's hand.

The dying human was my age, Nessa's age. Is this what it would have looked like if Nessa died? Blinking at her poor figure, I reached into my pocket, pulling out a MiraSalv med pouch, an invention of my parents. Now was as good a time as any to waste a packet or two.

Tossing it in their direction, I walked away. I knew, sooner or later, the woman would find it and know that it was meant to save her companion. Not that I really cared.

War and Peace

I rested alone in my air-conditioned room, staring at the brown ceiling. It had been a week since the victory dinner, and I was running out of time. On occasion, bounty hunters dragged their feet, if they were low on job opportunities, but this was too long. People were beginning to get suspicious.

So, hiding from prying eyes, I stayed in the room.

My abode was designed for a slaver. The area was plush, soft chairs and silk clothes, air conditioning, endless refreshments. But even with this, it was almost a relief when a soft knock came to the door.

Swinging my boots off the couch, I stepped to the door. I opened it to a badge from the World Authority Association.

I blinked, glancing over the average looking man behind the emblem, apparently some sort of undercover cop. I could feel my lips curve downwards with doubt. "You do realize your insignia will get you killed around here?"

He lifted one side of his lips dryly. "Officer Dallas Smith, Ms. Shandra Lux."

A NewAmerican. And he knew who I was. This could not be good. "What do you want?"

His smile vanished. "I don't have good news. I'm investigating a flight that crashed nearby. Believers were the ones involved, but it'll make the

World Authority Association look bad if we don't sort this out. Seth, the caretaker, found me, and asked me to show you the evidence. He said he didn't want to come himself. He said you were too hopeful."

My breath caught. "The evidence?"

He turned away. "I should just get this over with." He took a trinket out of his pocket. "There was a pyre, where they buried the dead."

I froze in place. I felt a rising desperation burn through me. This officer had to be mistaken.

"It's likely that Stroben had her killed, but it's also possible that she died when the plane went down." He shrugged unhappily. "Either way, this is all that's left of her. Take heart in the fact her burial was according to her customs. She was sent to her afterlife in a formal Believer funeral pyre." He pressed a necklace into my hands. "It's something all Believers wear. She would want you to have it."

"I know what a Believer medallion is," I murmured, my thoughts sluggish. Nessa couldn't just die. That wasn't who she was. She was supposed to live, to be healthy and happy, and okay.

I felt it in my hands, the smooth wood, the small word, *Agape* carved with such care. It was so light, so small. How could something so little matter so much to her? This was her medallion. I... This was... It was just... I just... I was too late.

I fell into a daze, finding myself standing in the gardens of the castle, evening light reflecting off the walls. I was on the roof of the black obelisk, the two horns of the palace towering over the greenery. But at this level, there was a simple path between clipped bushes and trees. There was a small synthetic river flowing through, giving the area the feel of an oasis. Not that it mattered.

Dawn may have come and left. Days could have gone by, and I wouldn't have known the difference, or even cared. Hours, days, years. Meaningless.

I had been in denial, searching for reasons not to believe the NewAmerican officer. I was so heartbroken that I found it hard to breathe, hard to stand, hard to be. I was full of rage, so much so that I wanted to destroy everything for the sin of existing in a world where my friend did not.

But there was one thing left to do before I took my revenge. I had to say goodbye.

Being a Believer, she would like me to do that. I stood by a tree, one sprinkled with pink, rosy flowers. It had a blue luminescence to it, a reminder of the war, and it shook in the wind, floating petals falling like a beautiful rain.

A single tear slipping down my cheek, unbidden, as I stared at the flowers. She'd wanted one so badly, from some unnamed stranger, the man she'd been waiting her whole life for. She was friendly, happy, and so hopelessly interested in finding her soulmate. How was it possible that she never had the chance to find him?

As the water babbled in the background, words found their way onto my lips. "Nessa. I wish you'd found some great guy." I gagged at my own words.

I was not going to be so shallow in my goodbye. "What I mean is, you deserved the best in life. You could have had anyone for a friend, but you chose me. No one had ever come for me before. No one had ever been there for me. I was an orphan and an outcast. But every time I asked, you would be there. I needed you. I needed someone who cared."

I let myself slip onto the ground, off the path, folding my feet together, pulling at the grass that surrounded the garden. "Do you remember that time at the convention? You were invited because of your charm, me because of my money. But you didn't have a dress, so you came to my place before the event to pick out that silk gown. And you broke the Serens Original Vase." I laughed quietly. "That cost like a million UVs. But it was so ugly. You did me a favor."

"And then you were gone. You even told me you were leaving for the trip, and you told me not to worry. I said I was a terrible person at heart, that I wouldn't worry one bit." I bit the inside of my mouth. "I contacted the police and the World Authority Association. I paid endless investigators. I sifted through file after file on travel records, family relations. I bribed gang members and senators, just for a scrap of information. But nothing came of it but a flight number. I lost you, and I couldn't find you in time. I'm sorry."

The wind picked up, rustling the leaves as if Nessa was speaking back. It almost sounded as if she was trying to tell me that it was okay, that she knew I tried, and that she would never hold it against me.

It was as if she was saying goodbye, just one last time. It was as if she was reminding me that she missed me. It was as if she was reminding me that she missed her friend.

But instead of hearing her voice, a pain exploded inside of me, a fire that reached into my fingers, though my legs, overriding my brain. My head pounded with this suffering, the edges of my vision turning a deep red as I gritted my teeth. This agony torching my soul was not a burden I could carry alone. Stroben had to share this. Perhaps the loss of her Favored One would be the beginning of fair payment for her crime.

Vengeance

I stepped down the hallway in the servants' quarters, past the other slaves' housing. My prey would not be there, not in the evening. This late, the scandal would be too great. I just hoped he was in his own quarters, rather than serving at some late-night meeting.

I found myself standing before a single door. The design of the doorway suggested this was a solitary room, accommodating a single slave. He had been given a great honor, not having companions to share his dorm with.

I contemplated kicking the door down, but there was a simpler way. I knocked.

There was the sound of movement and the soft tap of footsteps before the door opened wide. My target stood before me. His hair was sloppy, standing straight up on one side, and he had the imprint of a pillow across his cheek. He wore a thin, threadbare brown sweater with holes in it, grey pants. There was still the tattoo on his face.

Even with these accents, his toned arms curved flawlessly, his broad shoulders overshadowed by his sharp jaw. His eyes, splashes of green and brown, were as bright as ever. Even his confusion, a tired vulnerability, added to his striking aura. It didn't seem fair that he was this handsome, even when he'd just woken up.

He blinked at me, exhausted, his brain still waking. Wisely, however, he stayed silent.

"Stroben has offered you as a server at my celebration, as part of my payment."

He took a step back, crossing his muscular arms, lifting a skeptical eyebrow. "You must have made an impressive kill to have been given such a reward."

I cocked my head to the side. "Are you questioning me?"

"Of course not. That would be above my station." His sarcasm was well hidden in his monotonous words. "After all, you have the request papers in order, I'm sure." He pursed his lips together expectantly.

I laughed. If he wanted to play this way, I would, too. "You know, I'm not sure I have them. Perhaps I should contact Stroben directly. And while I'm at it, you can explain where you were last night."

"No one would contact Stroben for such a—" His skin paled in fear as my words sunk in. He straightened his arms out. "My apologies. I didn't mean to quest-question—" He swallowed hard, his face flushing with frustration. Finally, he dropped to his knees, the thudding sound echoing around the room. "It's not my place to question a superior. I was in error, and I will be able to serve. Can I have a moment to prepare, Hunter Storm, or would you rather I served as I am?" He gestured to his torn shirt.

I did not care what he died wearing, but giving him time before his death seemed right. "You'll want to prepare for this."

He nodded quickly, getting up, pushing the door until it was left barely ajar. He wanted privacy, but to close the door on someone like me, with my status and power, would be a show of disrespect to a social superior.

I pushed the door open again, just in time to see him step behind a dressing wall at the other end of the room. He was out of view, tossing his sleepwear onto the bed as he changed, unaware of my invasion.

As I waited for him, I took in his room. He had a bed, a mattress, even a small pillow. Across from this structure, there was a dresser, one drawer slightly opened. On display, there was a single mirror.

Swiftly, he pulled back a panel. He was now shirtless. He was frowning, wearing expensive pants made of black leather, black straps across each wrist. For a moment, I was once again caught off guard by his manicured features and curving muscles. It took Stroben's symbol across his chest to remind myself of my disinterest.

Stepping to the mirror, too lost in his own world to take note of my presence, he leaned forward, swiping a comb through his hair. He reached into a drawer and put a small necklace in his pocket. After a moment's pause, he worked through his locks again, concentrating as he stared at his reflection. As I took in his unknowing air, I felt a small amount of guilt. It wasn't his fault he was favored. But then, none of this was Nessa's fault, either.

After a few heartbeats of focus, he saw my reflection, my red armor, my tied brown hair, my burning brown eyes, in the glass. He jumped, his jaw dropping in a reflex of fear. Whipping his head back, he looked to me, surprise evident.

"Problem?"

"N-no. I'm sorry. I just… just didn't realize you were there. I'm sorry." He turned back to the mirror. His fingertips still gripped the comb, but his hands were now quivering.

If he continued in this state, he'd poke his eyes out. "You look good enough." My voice stilled his hands. "Let's go." Hearing his bare feet follow me, I stepped out the door.

As we walked down the hall, a woman stepped out of the other dorm. I tensed, ready for a fight. But it was the server who had been with the sick girl.

"Thank you." She threw her arms around him suddenly, tears streaming down her face, over her slave tattoo. "Thank you. I knew you could do it."

Aware of the breach she had committed, he pulled away from her. "Slave," he whispered, tilting his head in my direction. "Get ahold of yourself." I smiled. His fear was a refreshing reminder of my control of the situation.

She ignored him, still crying. "Irene got the medication. I know you had something to do with it. You saved her life. Thank you."

As he shook his head, a drop of sweat dripped down his neck. "I didn't do anything. Stroben didn't listen to me. And this is not at all appropriate. Leave us, now." With his show of leadership, he pushed himself away from her.

Remembering herself, she flinched. Instantly, she dropped to her knees, directing her attention to me. "Forgive me. I lost myself. I have no excuse."

"You're not the first one." I was not going to let this woman ruin my plan, especially after her show of disrespect. Talking out of turn like that, around a free woman, was pure idiocy. Not that this was the worst infraction she had. "And I'm sure you have no excuse for yesterday, either."

The woman bowed her head to the floor, pulling her hands over her head protectively.

The Favored One stiffened beside me. "If I may," he whispered. "If you are speaking of the other night, the infraction was mine. She had no control over my actions. I am solely to blame. And she is the lowest tier of slave. She is not a Favored One, and she is not worth your time."

I held his gaze for a long moment. He'd offered himself as punishment, instead of this woman. Pity struck me. He'd be easier to kill if he weren't so noble. Even so, while trying to protect his friend, this slave had given me an easy escape from this situation.

I allowed for a silence as I pretended to consider his words.

"If you leave her be, I would take it as a favor." His voice trembled. He could easily be killed, just for that single sentence of disloyalty. He swallowed, and in a short moment, I realized his reality. He wasn't worried about a beating. He thought I was going to kill the girl. And unknown to him, he was going to receive the punishment he thought was reserved for her.

I glanced at her for a hard moment, jutting my chin towards her door. "Server, you have three seconds to leave my presence. I would also suggest hiding from me for the rest of your life."

She nodded, skittering away in a moment of mercy that would not last. After all, I did have a murder to commit.

I led the Favored One away from the slave quarters. Walking up the stairs, we reached the main floor. I paused, pondering how to best exact revenge. Confused, the Favored One gestured to the next floor. I ignored him.

"We aren't going to my quarters. That is not where this celebration is."

He turned back to me, confusion in his features. "We're not? Where are we going, then?"

"That depends. Where's Stroben, right now?"

"She's in a late meeting with a few other Brokels, probably. In the throne room, where the execution was." He folded his arms. "I strongly suggest we avoid this floor. No matter what we're doing, if you interrupt her, she'll kill us both."

I allowed for a twisted grin. He knew I'd lied to him, and that he wasn't going to a celebration. But he hadn't figured out the whole story. "Of the two of us, I am not the one who should be worried."

He lifted his chin.

"Firstly, my name is not Storm. It's Lux."
Shandra Lux, not that he needed to know.

He tilted his head, confusion in his brow. "You
wish me to refer to you as Lux?"

"No. that's who I am."

"As you wish." His voice was a thread, his eyes
searching me for some clue of where this was
headed. His hand absentmindedly went to his chest,
over Stroben's brand.

It was about time he received the answers he was
looking for. "Have you noticed, slave, how much
attention Stroben gives you?"

I waited for a reply, so he nodded once,
hesitantly. "Hunter Lux, I am the Favored Slave."

"The others don't even get medicine, but you?
You get a mirror, a pillow. You eat at her table. You
get to break rules, steal food, visit your girlfriends."

His face drained. "This is about Irene?"

"Oh, not at all." I struck out suddenly, moving
my leg behind his knee, tripping him, sending him
to the ground. "This is about Stroben, and what she
took from me." I kicked at him, but he moved, and
my boot only scuffed by his shoulder.

His hand went to his arm for a moment as he
curled into himself.

"Get up and fight," I spat, finally finding an
outlet. "I'm going to end you, just like she did with
Nessa."

He didn't even try to follow my demand.
Instead, he remained unmoving, one arm

protectively placed over his face and neck. "I'm sorry. I'm sorry. I shouldn't have spoken to them. I had no right. I should know my place."

"This isn't about her. I hate you." I tore his hands away and shoved his face into the stone ground. "I hate Stroben." I grabbed him by his hair, pulling him up against the wall. "I even hate myself." I punched the wall next to him, feeling a burning sensation flow through my hand as the slave stared at me, quaking. "Now fight me."

"I can't, I can't. Please." He pulled himself away, kneeling into the wall. "Please. You're Stroben's guest. An Unaffiliated. My social superior. I can't fight you. I'm not supposed to even look at you." Directing his eyes downward once more, he choked. "I can't fight you."

"I don't care about your rules." I grabbed his bruised arm, pulling him to me as he locked his jaw. "This is about Stroben."

I wanted her to be here for this. I wanted her to see me kill him. I wanted to see the horror in her eyes as I took this Favored One from her. I wanted to see her rage at being stolen from like this. I wanted her to know that I was the cause of it. "Move." I demanded, pressing a heat-ray gun against his head. He complied. "Start walking. Take a left here. To the conference chambers."

He choked in realization. "Whatever you want from Stroben, you won't get it." As he moved down the hallway, his speech was nasally as blood dripped from his broken nose. "She... I'm a slave. I'm nothing. She won't care. I'm worthless."

I gestured him towards the door. "You underestimate yourself. She lets you eat at her table."

"You don't understand. I'm a slave. I'm nothing to her. I'm nothing to anyone."

I snickered. "On the contrary. She murders others blindly, but when you poison her, you're left untouched. She could have picked anyone, but she chose you. You're everything to her. That makes you everything to me." I opened the door. With a swift kick, jabbing my foot to the small of his back, I sent the slave flying into the room. He crashed to the floor before his master, landing in the center of a mural of her flaming tree.

Though I could not see into the room, I heard the meeting come to a sudden close, silence falling, the air dead as Stroben stood. "My pathetic Favored One, you will be punished."

The slave kept his head down as I stepped in. At a table in the corner, there were Stroben and two other Brokels, with a collage of bodyguards. Among this crowd was the lethal woman, and the scowling man.

"Oh, don't worry about punishment. I can do that for you." I drew closer to the slave, placing my boot on the side of his face, pressing his cheek into the painting on the floor.

The slave grunted.

"What is the meaning of this?" Stroben demanded, folding her arms. The female bodyguard drew a laser pistol. The other Brokels watched the interaction with mild interest.

"The meaning? You took the only thing I ever cared about. I'm going to do the same to you."

She shook her head in seething anger. The woman with the weapons removed her safety with a soft click, but Stroben made a small gesture. "I paid you fairly for your kill." She was worried the slave, her property, might get hurt in a fight.

I laughed, insane. I almost sounded like Stroben. "This is not about the kill. This is about the plane of Believers who crashed. You took the survivors, and you killed them. You killed the only person in this world worth saving." Kneeling, I pressed the gun to the man's head.

Stroben paused, her voice softening as she flipped from one extreme emotion to the next. "You knew one of them?"

"I was loyal to her. Nothing more."

"Her?" The Brokel paused, glancing to her bodyguard, the one with the perpetual scowl. He took out a data screen. "Was there a female survivor?"

After some silence, the bodyguard found what he was looking for. "Four survivors. Male, thirty-nine. Leg trauma. Died in the med bay. Male, twenty. Minor injuries. Employed for sports entertainment until termination. Male, seven. Lacerations. Died on route. Male, thirty. Employed for sports entertainment until termination. There wasn't a girl."

"Do you think I care what your records say? You killed her." Even if Nessa died in the crash, it was still Stroben's fault. "Let's see what your records say about this."

Slowly, with a callous power, I hooked my elbow around the slave's neck, forcing him to look up. I wanted Stroben to see the light leave his eyes. I took in the shape of the slave before me as he twitched his arms to his pocket. At first, I assumed it was some pathetic attempt to free himself, a reach for a weapon. My hand was there first.

It wasn't a weapon. I froze, glancing at the trinket. It was a pendant carved with the word *Eros*. A Believer's Medallion?

Just like Nessa. He was like her. My cold resolve to murder him faltered.

Stroben lifted a hand, attempting to calm me. "He's a Believer in Love, like your friend. They were all Believers on that plane. And he is, too. Are you willing to kill a Credo Brother?"

I was suddenly aware of the slave's face, of the bruised imprint of my boot on the side of his cheek. I—I glimpsed up at the crowd before me. I hadn't been shot yet because the slave was alive, mostly unhurt, and I was too close to him to be sure he stayed that way.

I hadn't thought about what my plan had been after he died, but the situation was now shifting. Not killing this man had huge, frustrating, life-threatening implications. But… Nessa. This man could have been her Brother, her friend, her anything. I wanted badly for her to live. This felt like a memorial to her own life.

My options were seriously limited as I crouched, surrounded by Stroben's flames. Shooting at the Brokel, actively attempting to kill her, would be a sure way to die fast. Staying in the current situation was also dangerous. The only option I was coming up with was to simply run.

If I wanted to stay alive while fleeing, I had to keep him close to me. I forced him to his feet, pulling him in front of me like a shield, backing out of the room. But as I did so, Stroben issued one cold command. "Bring her to me."

The hunter had become the hunted.

Flight from Egypt

"Run." I shoved him forward. "My transport. Behind the kitchens."

He bolted, terrified. I followed silently. We tore through hallways and corridors, transitioning away from the rich areas designed to impress, into small slave paths. The sound of his bare feet echoing off the walls was followed by the too-close footsteps of the predators.

As we reached the pantries, I dashed through the darkened area, but the slave staggered behind me. The wounds. The broken nose. Not even the adrenaline rush was enough to keep him going.

"Keep running, or you die," I hissed. "How many more will follow us?"

"Just the two." He took a deep breath. "Koren and Ceba. Professionals. Slave recovery." His pace slower, he continued. As we reached a door at the end of the hallway, they appeared behind us. The woman began shooting, beams from the lasers burning past us.

The woman was shooting to kill. In fact, she was aiming for the slave. It made sense, suddenly, why this slave was willing to comply with my demands.

As we left the hallway, we dove into the night, our path lit by the moon. I pointed to an all-terrain vehicle, a transport often driven before the Credo Wars. Being a TerrieV 29 model, it had the option of an open ride, a tarp thrown up like a ceiling. I thought for a moment about cranking up the walls to give me more protection, but that would be a precious minute I didn't have.

When I came to the castle, I thought it might be useful to have my own transport, and the leisure of this creation was just too much for me to pass up. Rather than the speeders that were common, I had a thing for old school transport. But now, having two elite killers behind me, I wished I had chosen something that offered more protection than the open ride. And thinking of putting up the side walls for protection would have been a great idea, too.

Diving in, I flipped on the iris scan to start the engine as the slave climbed into the passenger side. As I grabbed the wheel, a thought struck me. I wasn't planning on bringing him with me. I hadn't thought this all through. He was a slave. He told me at the meal. He had a tracker in his arm. Stroben could look up our location. She could find us. She could hunt us down. She could see our every move. I had to get rid of him. Or I had to tear it out of him.

MiraSalv paste could heal that wound, right? "Your transmitter. Where is it?"

He shook his head, his hand covering his wrist. "Please, no. I'll die."

I glanced to where the two killers would arrive, and I knew we were running out of time. Pulling a knife out of my belt, I ran a blade across his wrist, cutting through his wristband as I sliced into the skin.

He shoved himself away, almost falling out of the car, but I put my forearm across his neck, shoving him back into the chair, keeping him locked in place. Even so, hunting for the tracker amidst the ever-growing spray of blood was not working.

As I worked on the wrist, the two killers came flying from around a corner, the woman already shooting at us. Lethal projectiles sprayed around me, barely missing us. Between the moonlight and the gunshots, there was no way I would be able to find the tracker in time. I let go of the slave, his wrist still gashed open. Transitioning, I gripped the wheel, shifting my car into gear, cursing the fact that this model didn't have autopilot.

I was speeding off, creating distance between us, but they were sure to catch up. I flew out over the packed sand dunes, not even leaving tire tracks behind me, cursing the full moon that night.

Barely out of shooting distance, I turned back to the slave. He stared at me, horrified, his torso drenched in red. "Your transmitter." He was going to have to be the one to get it out. I didn't have the time or the hands.

He lifted his unwounded hand to me, holding a small metal rod.

"You found it?" I asked dumbly. This was impressive. If he could handle taking out his own tracker, he was tougher than I thought.

"Koren and Ceba can track it." He dropped it on the sand of the desert as we sped by. "Can you… the blood? Stop it? Somehow?"

"Yeah. I've got a way." Granted, he may have already lost too much blood. "Med kit. In the back. Open it. Large white bottle." He followed my instructions, turning backwards in his seat to follow my commands. "There's blue gel inside. Apply it to your wrist, and make sure it covers the whole wound."

I looked over enough to see him struggle with the lid of the gel, performing the task without the use of his injured arm. But after a moment, he worked off the top, and smeared the MiraSalv across his skin.

The blood stopped instantly. He stared at his arm as if a miracle had befallen him. I allowed for a small smile. After all, it had been my family's invention that saved his life. "You'll need to wrap some sort of cloth around that," He stared at me, still bewildered by the drug. "It'll help the blood flow, but it still needs time to heal. Also, with the blood loss, you're minutes away from shock. There's an adrenaline shot. Med kit. In the plastic container. Left side."

The sound of a following engine cut into the silence. The two bodyguards were catching up.

With them gaining ground, we had no place to hide, just one packed dune after another. If I hadn't been distracted by the Favored One, his slower running, his arm, I could have had this all work out better.

I looked back, seeing a small shape in the distance. They had found me.

The slave's face was chalk white, and he was half conscious. "Two clicks west. Saltburn Sea. ATVs can do wet sand." He moaned as I turned west. "Breez 36, that's a speeder. Faster. Can't do water."

I raced towards the lake, seeing it grow in the distance. The two bodyguards only continued to gain ground. When they were within shooting distance, they made it clear. "Can you fire a gun, too?" Maybe this slave was full of surprises.

He shook his head. "Not steady."

He had a point. Weapons were hard enough, even before blood loss. "Fine, you drive." I let go of the wheel, jamming the accelerator into the on position. I climbed into the back of the TerrieV, taking out my gun.

I aimed at the speeder behind us, at the two bodyguards. Specifically, I was aiming for the man, the one who was driving. I shot. Their ship wavered, and I knew I had hit him. It wasn't a kill shot, but their transport slowed, giving us the lead we needed as we sped into the marshy sands. The Breez 36 wouldn't be able to catch us now. It just wasn't built for this terrain.

We continued, but they fell behind until they were out of sight. I knew renting this Terrie could only lead to good things.

After a great while of staring behind us, flinching at every new sound, I looked back to the slave. He was still driving, white knuckled, along the edge of the waters. "They still there?" he asked, his voice tight.

"They'll be back, but it's fine for now." I moved back to the front, striking his shoulder to move him out of my way. He flinched, drawn out of his trance. "Let me drive."

He let go of the wheel, climbing lethargically to his side, skin a sickly white in the moonlight. "I think-I think—I'm shaking?"

I glanced over to him as I took the wheel. The adrenaline shot had worn off, and now the blood loss was catching up to him.

"Synthablood," I said. "left compartment. It'll replenish you, but it'll also mess with your system. It'll knock you out for a while."

He nodded but didn't hesitate as he injected himself. In a moment, he slumped into his chair. Soon, the hum of the car and his light breathing were the only sounds as I drove through the night.

Terra Incognita

I looked over this desert, but it was constantly more of the same. Each mound was constructed of packed sand, all of which sparkled in the sunlight, giving a fluttering illusion of beauty, reaching out until the eye could see no more, just the tan of the sand and the jet blue of the sky.

"How does your arm feel?" I hadn't spoken for hours. We'd been driving in total silence since the day began, except to put up the shade canopy on the vehicle and to grab food and water throughout the day. With the dusk coming upon us once more, I was bored.

He started, uncurling from the position he'd taken for the last while, his hands leaving his broken nose. After a shallow breath, he pawed at his face. "What?"

"Your arm. The cut up one." I gestured to him with my free hand, not that letting go of the wheel would matter in this desert.

His fingers wrapped themselves over his bandage. "It's fine. It doesn't hurt much."

"Liar."

He bristled. "What would you rather I said?"

"The truth, *slave*." By virtue of his position, he shouldn't be mouthing off at me. I was tired. I hadn't completed my revenge. I was in no mood for this.

He shrunk, remembering his place. "It hurts. Badly. But I'm alive."

I accepted his words this time, but as the silence screamed in the space between us, I continued the conversation. "So, why'd you choose Eros?"

He paused. "What?"

"Your Believer Medallion. You chose Eros. Why?" Every Believer of love was given a medallion when they joined, and they chose which form of love they wished to carve into it.

"Oh. Eros. I just… I liked the sound of it."

I lifted an eyebrow, letting the expression speak for me. "You liked the sound of it?"

"Um, yeah." He coughed. "And I wanted to pledge myself to the Eros type of love."

"I see." I allowed for another long pause. "Which type of love is that?"

He took a long breath. "Eros. It's when you love somebody no matter what. And all that."

"Is it?"

"Yes."

"Hm. Agape is undying, heroic love. Philos is friendship. As for Eros? I could have sworn that Eros tends to be a physical, husband and wife type. Kissing and whatnot." I took a sarcastic breath. "But you're the Believer. Maybe I'm just wrong."

He grit his teeth, caught. "It's not—you're not—I just liked the word."

I slammed on the breaks, allowing the Terrie to skid in the packed sand.

"What are you, then? Besides a liar?" Why didn't I kill him in front of Stroben?

"Not a Believer. Stroben lied to you to get you to stop. If that's why you didn't blow my brains out, just kill me now."

I reached for my gun, pulling out the medallion. "Where did you get this, then?"

He glanced at the armament, but his eyes drew themselves over to the pendant. Finally, he hung his head. "It belonged to someone I cared about. She was captured with me."

"It's not yours? You stole it? Are you a liar and a thief?"

"No." His face scrunched. "We were captured together. I just—She was from the Serens."

I snorted. "That does not explain how you ended up here, with her medallion in your hands. You do know that it's part of their culture to keep their medallion. To take it from her, for you to have it? You're disgusting."

"No, I—" He wrapped his hand around his bandaged arm. "I swear, it's not like that. She had to take her pilgrimage. It's a Believer thing. But also, illegal. I thought going with her would somehow make it safer. I was an idiot.

"We boarded a plane with twenty other believers. And we went down near the Saltburn Sea. I think someone opened fire on us. Stroben's men were the first to find us. Echo was injured. Everyone was battered. We couldn't fight back. Minutes after we were brought into the palace, Ceba brought us before Stroben. Our pilot said something, so Koren started beating on him. I just wasn't used to violence like that, yet. I spoke up."

"You *are* bad at keeping your mouth shut," I mused.

"I told him to stop. Koren was about to attack me, but Stroben halted him. I think the fact I spoke caught her eye. That was when she—That's when I became her favorite dog. For a while, I fought her. But as long as I was Stroben's animal, I could make sure Echo had a safer job, make sure she was protected. I could even persuade Stroben, sometimes to do small things, feed the slaves a bit more. She sometimes let me steal food for them." Like when he took the bread.

He swallowed, conflicted, trying to keep his mouth shut after his many admissions. After only a short moment, he continued. "She allowed me to get close enough to kill her. She was a maniac, believe me. I had to stop her, and I didn't see another way. I tried to poison her, it's true. In return, she killed Echo." His voice cracked.

"Echo. Your Believer." Like Nessa was my Believer.

"She was perfect. In the Serens, she had this incredible skill, like she could get anyone or anything to like her. You should have seen the way she worked with animals. It was like she didn't care that the World Authority Association oppressed her people, because she had something better than the government could ever have." Just like Nessa.

"And you should have seen her after we were caught. I thought it would break her, but it didn't. Nothing did. She knew that Stroben was destroying me, but she never gave up. We weren't allowed to see each other, but she found ways to write small notes on scraps, or to pass by me in the halls. She kept reminding me there was still hope. She knew how messed up I'd been, and she never gave up on me. Never once. She was my everything."

He had a Believer that he cared about. His Believer had been killed by Stroben. He had been lost without her. "You loved her."

He curled his knees back to his chin again, his voice becoming tight in a sudden change of tone. "Yes."

The space between us was filled with thoughts neither of us felt the need to share. I started the car again, and we drove through the darkness. "Got a name?"

He curled up once more. "A name? I thought I said it was Echo."

"Your name."

"Yes, I have a name." He gave a soft laugh. "Do you have a name? I know it's not Luna Storm. If you were her, you'd have way more of a bloodlust, and you would never allow me to continue breathing. And you'd be way better at a getaway. And Lux is a family name. That's who you belong with, not who you are."

My lips twitched. "Shandra. My name is Shandra Lux."

"Shandra," he whispered softly, trying it out.

"And if I'm not like Storm, what am I like?"

He pursed his lips together, his tone suddenly wary. "You're dangerous, and a poor planner. But you aren't insane, not like a bounty hunter. I know you noticed me during that celebration. I saw you. When you showed up at my door, I thought you were just messing with me. But you were lying through your teeth. Then you…" He rubbed his jaw, still bloody from the time I attacked him. "I thought you were going to kill me." He paused. "Why didn't you? Why did you save me? Was it really because you thought I was a Believer?"

Yes. It was. But I wasn't sure I wanted to tell him that. Instead, I lifted an eyebrow at him. "What do you think?"

He chewed the inside of his cheek. "I think…" he paused for a while as the stars continued blooming above us. "Underneath everything you try to be, you might be a good person. Maybe."

I laughed. "And for a moment there, I actually thought you were intelligent. But then, you are a Favored One."

He blushed. "That's not—I'm not just a Favored One. I also know a lot about transports. I just… I don't know. That's not all I'm good for." He paused for a long moment. "Wait, are you—looking for a Favored Slave?"

Was I looking for a pet? I laughed. "Trust me, we'll part ways soon."

"You… but you just…." His eye scrunching as if he'd been struck, he let out a sound of frustration. "Don't sell me on the markets. Stroben will find me in a heartbeat. She'll let Koren and Ceba practice on me. They're too good to let me die quickly. I can't do that. Keep me. I can be amazing. Loyal. Handsome. Anything." His shoulders lifted into fake confidence. "I can make you happy. I swear."

I sniggered. "Wow. The humility."

"No. They just had me on a strict diet, fibers, starches, whatever built muscle. Stroben wanted a Favored One who was nice to look at, so that's what they made me. They had me work out for three hours a day." his voice wavered. "I mean, she had exact specifications. She wanted me to be lean, but all muscle. I was physically strong, of course, so they injected me with an electro-version, so they could shock me if I got out of hand. But if you don't like my looks, I can be emotionally supportive. I could be a companion, a loyal follower. I just can't get caught by Stroben. Not again. Don't sell me."

"In NewAmerica, we're not in the habit of selling humans." But what was I going to do with him? "If we continue north like this, we'll get to NewIstanbul. Do you know the area?"

"NewIstanbul? I think so."

"It's on the line between three of the four quadrants of the world, The Believers of Power, the Believers of Serenity, and The Free Zone. When we get there, I'll buy you a ticket and fake papers. You can go wherever you want, and you can leave." That way, he'd never find his way back to Stroben.

"Free?" Fear was etched into his features. "She will find me." He shook his head, holding his bandage close to his chest. "No. I know Stroben. I can't fight her. She'll find me. I need somebody to protect me. I can't be free. Where would I even go? I don't know anyone out there."

I lifted an eyebrow. Freedom was something he should have been excited about. But then again, maybe it did make sense. After years of having every action planned for him, having a million choices was a bit much.

But maybe freedom was exactly what he needed. Maybe nothing less than that would give him the will to escape Stroben.

We drove on in the silence, minutes turning to hours as we crossed the endless sand. The tranquility of it was a dramatic change from our flight. It was hard to accept that I was relatively safe. I kept expecting the slave catchers to appear after the next sand dune. But the sand came and went, and Koren and Ceba made no appearance as the time drained away and the sun set, giving way to a cold darkness.

After midnight, there was a soft scraping sound, like sandpaper against a metal, and then a scratching, just louder than the hum of my engine, came to my ears.

I honed in on it, wondering if I was overstressed and imagining things. Maybe my brain was looking for problems, over-panicked by the knowledge that the two slave hunters were after us. Maybe I was more sleep deprived than I thought. Maybe I was—

No. The sound was there. It was getting worse.

Whatever it was, it was now scuffing against the sand that we were driving on.

Worried that it would simply snap off, whatever it was, I slowed the car to a halt. I had to see what was going on, even if there wasn't much I could do about it. As I moved, the Favored One shifted, somehow also aware of the change.

He opened his eyes, glancing to me questioningly. His face looked different—he'd set his nose.

"Stay in the car," I hissed, stepping out.

As I stepped up to the front of my vehicle, I realized a profound truth. With owning MiraCorp, I had enough money to pay any mechanic in the city. As a result, I had no idea how this contraption worked. In fact, I wasn't even sure this part of the car was called a hood.

As I stared in the dark, clueless, at the machine before me, the Favored One grabbed at the door on his side, slipping out. He clung to the front of the car, still drained by the blood loss and the escape.

"How does it look?"

I frowned at him. "Get back into the car."

He squinted at me through exhausted eyes. "I don't want to walk to NewIstanbul. It's a long enough journey by transport. About a week by foot. I don't want to die of dehydration as we hike." He tapped the metal of the TerrieV. "Fill me in. What do we have?"

I paused, surprised by this shift in him. He had an aura of confidence that I hadn't seen before. He wasn't cowering, and he wasn't afraid of me, and he didn't care that we were running from Stroben.

I pointed to the contraption. "The car is making a sound."

He folded his arms. "Can you be more specific? Or is that all we have to work with?"

"Something's dragging."

He nodded and crouched, positioning himself down by the wheels. But before he had the chance to reach under or investigate the problem, his face whitened, and he cupped his head in his arms.

He moved too fast. "It's a side-effect of blood loss. You might get real nauseous, see stars, all that. You need to take it easy."

"Nausea," he mumbled. "Definitely nausea. And d-dizzy. Feeling that, t-too." After a moment, however, it passed, and he glanced up at me. "Right. Okay. Do—do you have any sort of illuminator? Or a retro tool, like a flashlight?"

"An illuminator." I grabbed one off my belt, tossing it too him.

He let it fall into the sand and slowly picked it up, taking his time as he glanced under. "You do have something hanging here." He reached a hand under. "Your engine splash shield disconnected on the left side. It looks like it wore through the bolt in the middle."

I had no idea what he was talking about. "Is it a serious problem?"

"In this terrain? Yes. It helps keep the sand from getting in the engine. It runs on Classic. Which doesn't do well with sand." He reached his hand under the machine once more. "But it could also be an easy fix. If you've got spare wires, or synthaglue, or anything of that sort, I could patch it up."

I pressed my lips together. "You could patch it up." I tried the words in my mouth, and I did not like them. On the one hand, this man could destroy the engine if I let him work on it, on purpose or by accident. Or he could fix the... thing. The thing that was broken.

"How would a Favored One know how to patch up a TerrieV 29?"

My sentence brought him back to his old self and he glanced at his wounded arm. "I just—I just—I thought I could help." His cheeks flushed. "I'm not worthless. I mean, I am. But I can—There are things I'm good at. I know mechanics."

"What if you make it worse?"

"It's just a splash shield. It's an easy fix. I could—I could tell you how to do it, and you could fix it yourself."

I paused, shaking my head. In all honesty, if he broke the car and stranded us out here, he would be trapped, too. Koren and Ceba would bring him back. He probably wanted to get moving again as much as I did. Sabotaging our transport would make no sense.

60

I moved to the back of my car. I popped open the vehicle and grabbed a package of the glue, and threw it beside him. "You do it. But if you mess this up, I'll hand you to Stroben myself. Got it?"

"Yes." He inched forward. He was lying on the ground, his back against the sand, his head centimeters from the underside of the hood. His left arm reached under, his right resting on the front, almost touching his forehead. His brow furrowed in focus as he turned his head to see what he was working on. "Hold the light for me? I can't do it myself." He grabbed for the glue.

As he worked, I stared at his chest, the light barely illuminating the sprawling flames drawn across it. The greenery and the fire were smudged into a blur of paint, but the brand was still obvious. "The light. Higher," He murmured. I turned it, and his chest was shrouded, the darkness erasing the image.

As time passed by, he grew in confidence, and this new version of him appeared again. It was as if this was what he was meant for, and he'd just remembered his true calling.

He spent a while fiddling with two black strips. He must have been trying to connect them together, but his hands weren't slim enough, and he wasn't close enough at all. After watching him struggle for some time, I finally offered, "Why don't you just crawl under the car?"

He laughed, actually laughed, and then he smiled at me. His smile was handsome.

"I'll answer your question if you answer mine."

"It wasn't a questi—

"*Why* is a question word. I will answer you if you answer me."

"Just answer me."

He sighed. "Crawling under a car is idiotic and dangerous, without professional stabilizing tools." He struggled against the black... thing... under the car for a bit. "Having a car fall on you is not super fun."

I grunted noncommittally.

"My turn." He said, pressing on. "How does someone so rich that they can buy an antique transport end up doing the legwork to find a Believer?"

I froze, a bit surprised by his question. No one but Nessa was close enough that they asked about me, about the choices that I made, about what got me to where I was now.

I didn't owe this man any answers, and I was a cold human being, but it was true that I would never see him again. I had nothing to lose. He just— he was like Nessa. Maybe he listened, like she always did. "You're right about me being rich. I own MiraCorp, a medical company in America. I did pay about ten investigators to hunt her down. But whoever hurt Nessa, someone working for Stroben probably, was working against me, messing with every investigator I hired. They all came up empty. I had to go it alone."

He nodded. "I need the light over here," he mumbled. "You did that all for your Believer. You must have some extreme friendships."

I shook my head, not that he noticed. "Yeah. I didn't have many friends. But she was always there for me. She always told me that'd I'd change the world one day."

He snorted as he finished gluing the object that was dragging. "Who's to say she's wrong?"

"The bruise on your face. The fact I was going to shoot you. The fact I put you in mortal danger. Trust me, she was wrong."

He was silent for a long moment. "You also helped me escape. It may not have been your intention, but I'm away from Stroben." He pulled his hands away from the car. "Even if this isn't permanent, if I get brought back tomorrow, at least I had this moment, right now."

The vehicle repaired, he stood once more. "It'll get us to NewIstanbul. But once you're there, you're going to want to have it looked at."

I nodded, directing him back into the Terrie. "We still have while to go. Don't get your hopes up that we'll reach the city." I climbed into my side, turning the car back on, and continued the journey.

As moments morphed into hours, my shoulders drooped, my eyes sore. Exhaustion built in me as I stared at the monotonous flash of the sand dunes. With sunrise lighting the sky I finally shut off the engine, my eyelids heavy. If I waited much longer, it would be too hot to sleep at all.

Granted, it was biting cold now. I hated this sandy, predictable, unchanging desert.

I reached back into the back of the Terrie, pulling out an extra jacket. It had a distinct footprint on it from when I stood back there, taking shots at the slavers, but I didn't care. I wrapped the cloth around my shoulders, overwhelmed by the frosty air.

In a strange wave of empathy, I glanced to the slave, wondering how he found the will to sleep in this harsh temperature.

He was curled awkwardly in his seat, back facing me, his legs pulled up to his chin, shivering in his slumber. His hands were covering his swollen nose, which was probably still throbbing. I could see his tense back muscles, pulled taunt with a constant stress he could not shake even as he escaped into his dreams.

And even at rest, he looked… Manicured. Doted. Pet like.

I took in the toned and unprotected body of his, beat into perfection, simply because his master wanted it. I took in the way his body shone in the moonlight, sharp curves and turns accenting his arms and torso. I took in the way his wavy brown hair fell about his head, tousled from the journey.

I wondered how he could be this trusting. He was sleeping as I, the being who crushed his face into the ground, sat beside him.

But then, perhaps this was not trust. Perhaps he had slept in a den of horror for so long that he no longer knew what it was to feel safe.

There was a wave rising in me, some sort of sorrow. I felt for this man, for his lot in life, for his submissive ways, so clearly not his true nature, for his lack of freedom, for his stripped dignity.

I reached out and draped my jacket across his shoulders.

NewIstanbul

"Welcome to NewIstanbul." My pathetic displays of emotion long past, I flashed an almost bored smile. "Here's where you get off. If you head into the Serens, Stroben's tree of fire won't even be legal. Head to NewAmerica, and they'll hunt her down for you."

The Favored One swallowed, unamused by my comments. Instead, he was staring at the sector, a marketplace surrounding us. There were people selling clothes and rugs, rich shoppers in fine colors, the sugary smell of dried fruits mixing in the air. The warm wind blew a wave of sand into the faces of the unperturbed shoppers.

The Favored One's attention was locked on a woman. She was wearing a thin pink dress, accented by gold chips and a single sleeve. On her dress, there was a brand of a ram, another Brokel. It took a long glance for me to notice that she wore the same tattoo. She was a Favored Slave, too. She stopped, reaching for a scarf on display, asking for a price. A handsome vendor spoke back to her, suggesting something as he drew out a few more cloths to interest her. After a long moment, he pushed a silver shawl forward as he spoke. In response to his suggestion, she laughed, innocently smiling at her charmer.

The slave in my Terrie bunched his muscles, suddenly taunt. A man dressed in silks crossed in front of our car, heading to the girl. Within moments of reaching her, he lashed his muscled arm out, striking her across the face.

The vendor recoiled, explaining something indistinguishable.

"She needs to take full responsibility," The Favored One hissed in a thin voice. "She has to do it now, or her owner will kill that man."

She knelt down, crying into her hands, pouring out words we couldn't hear. Another slave came up, carrying fresh produce and dried meat. The master turned, staring at the new slave for a long moment. Then, he stabbed the newcomer in the shoulder.

Materials crashed to the ground, scattering as the slave fell. The master stepped away with nonchalance. "Not a fatal wound." My Favored One watched as the girl in pink tore her clothes, wrapping a bandage around her companion's bleeding shoulder. The vendor attempted to help, but the woman shoved him away, waving fearfully at him, gesturing for him to leave. "She's lucky. Stroben would have tortured them all."

"Yeah." The Favored One's paranoia was beginning to make sense.

We watched silently as the two slaves gathered themselves, the Favored One crying as the other bled. They stepped in line behind the master as he disappeared into the crowd, the three vanishing into the masses. Soon he was replaced by others, free beings, persons with dark skin, light, Believers of Serenity, Believers of Power, men, women, rich, poor, good, evil. There were people selling goods, shouting at any passerby who would notice them. There were rich beings and politicians, rushing off angrily. There were families, fathers holding young children as they navigated through the marketplace.

The Favored One stared at the crowd, overwhelmed. "Got family anywhere?" I suggested. "I'll send you back to them, if you want. That's usually a good place to start."

He grimaced as he glanced down, his nose still swollen. "I don't have family left, no." he said after a long silence. "I... she... the medallion. She was my last connection to the outside world. We were engaged before we were taken to the palace."

I reached into my pocket, returning the charm that had stayed his execution, tossing it to him.

"Thank you," he whispered, holding it once more.

"Eros," I said, reading the word on the token. "Crazy love."

He cleared his voice. "I'll go to Eastern Seren. Her family was from the Serens. Maybe I'll try to find them."

"Nine hundred in cash enough to get you there?"

He shrugged, but I knew that my figure was right. I drew out the UVs.

"One more thing." I said, holding it out. "You got a name?"

"I'm just the Favored One."

I hardened my expression. "You weren't always that way. You were a mechanic or something, right? You must have had a name, once."

"Yeah. Once." He rubbed the bandage on his wrist, suddenly uncomfortable.

"You don't lose a name."

He shrugged. "That name belonged to a guy who didn't… do… what I did back there. It belonged to a better man who didn't… I'm not that man anymore. Not after what I've done."

I handed him the cash. "Leave the brokenness behind. Leave Stroben in the dust and go find a family." He needed to find a name again, too.

He took a breath, stepping out of the vehicle.

His tattoo slightly faded, he stood, wearing the jacket I had given him the night before. The collar of the top was pulled up to hide stains of Stroben's brand. If it wasn't for the tattoo still sprawled across his face, he would have fit in well with the hodgepodge that surrounded him.

"It's Leon," he said, turning back one last time before he walked into the chaos that was the unknown. "My name was Leon."

He vanished into the crowd, a slave turned free who was given his second chance at life.

If I hadn't known myself any better, I would have said that I had done a good deed. But in my heart, I knew that I had just made sure Stroben's Favored One would never find his way back to the master I loathed. That would drive the Brokel insane. And the way I did it? Nessa would have been proud.

Part II Second Comings

Erroneous Reasoning

I sat in my car with a wide-brimmed hat. It was pushed down over my eyes, and I was scowling at the nothingness. I actually hadn't even moved the car, too lazy and bored to find the motivation. I was still here, in the marketplace, the civilians giving sufficient space to a person so high class that I owned my own transport.

I had been lightly sleeping, on and off, enjoying being in my TerrieV 29. Hours had passed since the slave left. Only now, I was beginning to realize that I had no idea what to do with the rest of my life.

Finding Nessa had been my sole purpose. I had hunted for her endlessly. Going back to NewAmerica was unnecessary, as my company basically ran itself. I had no friends and no family. The only other person I had gotten along with was the slave. Not that I actually cared about him.

Now he was gone too. I had nothing to do. I could sleep, parked lazily just outside of the city limits.

But the sound of incoming footsteps interrupted this leisure. Without removing the hat that covered my face, I focused. The intruder was male, likely, and had the size and build of the bodyguard, the slaver, who had tried to kill me.

In a cold moment of comprehension, I realized
that I only heard his footprints, and no others. If
the woman was around, I didn't know where she
was. I didn't like things I didn't know.

Feeling for the gun between my seat and the
passenger side, I softly removed the safety. When
the pair of feet stopped moving, standing yards
away from my beautiful car, I lifted the weapon.
My hat was still over my eyes, but I didn't need to
see him to kill him. "If you've got a death wish, I
can help you out. Otherwise, keep walking,
Beautiful."

"I've got a death wish."

It didn't sound like a slave catcher. I knew that
voice.

In a flash, I could picture him, my jacket over his
shoulder hiding his broad back and defined biceps,
features that would fade with time and happiness. I
used a single finger to push my wide brimmed hat
up an inch, looking over to the man before me.

I didn't lower my gun, but my demeanor shifted.
"What happened to your Seren plans?"

Leon held a cheap data screen out, a hopeful
brow accenting the green in his eyes. "I saw this. I
was wondering if it changed anything."

I glanced down at what he handed me as I put
my weapon away. It was a tablet from the news
circles. It was the World Authority Information
Outlet, and the headline was something about a
slave rights activist. They were a growing fad.
Apparently, the WAA government saw slavery as a

huge evil. Illegal, even. Which was ironic, because they treated Believers as less than slaves.

I scanned the page, bored by the words. It talked about an event that had gone down not long ago, where a nobody was taken from some rich, influential somebody. The reporter wasn't sure what the intent was, but he had gotten quotes from various people who hoped this unknown knight was a hero who would free the slaves, or a rights activist who would—

"Oh, they're talking about me kidnapping you," I said. The news had gotten out really fast, and they put an inaccurate and positive twist on it. I glanced to his swollen nose.

"They think you have a vendetta against the slave lords, that you're on our side. Or maybe you're a Freedom Dreamer." He looked into my eyes. "Are they right?"

A Freedom Dreamer. A slave rights activist? An extremist who put the rights of the worthless plebeians before himself? Someone who didn't run on revenge? "No," I said, watching his shoulders drift downward. "I smashed your face in. That makes it a safe bet to say that I'm not on your side."

His fingers found their way up to the bridge of his nose, where the bruise was already yellowing. "But then you helped me escape. You gave me enough money to start a new life."

"Mixed signals, you're right. But Leon, let me give you a tip. If someone puts a gun to the back of your head, kicks your face, or threatens to kill you, you should never come back to them."

He laughed. "Everyone tries to kill me. Koren and Ceba were paid to keep slaves in line, and they made me a target. And there was always punishment. Sometimes, Stroben would hurt me just because she was in a mood."

It was a good thing I got him out of there.

He mistook my expression of surprise for disbelief. "It's true. Well, I mean, when I needed a chastisement, they weren't allowed to do anything that would disfigure me. Who scars a dog? Even my handcuffs were padded to make sure they didn't leave a mark. Instead of bruises, they would bring me to a cell and inject me with this stuff—Deprov." He paused, suddenly, biting his lip. "Why did I just—I shouldn't have told you any of that."

I shrugged a single shoulder. "Sometimes, the things that hurt us just spill out." In terms of bad choices, talking this much was fine. Coming back to someone who broke his nose was less fine. An annoying wave of guilt struck me.

He continued, unsure what to make of my silence. "So... I realized that I had escaped. I was like that girl in the marketplace. She got away clean, no marks, no bruises, nothing. But her slave-companion got hurt. I could have boarded a plane to Seren. But the other slaves? They're not even Favored Ones. They're still back there, enduring that." He took a breath. "Maybe you are on our side.

Or maybe you're not. Maybe you just hate Stroben."

"If I were you, I'd go with that option."

"Then come back with me and teach her a real lesson. Hit her where it hurts. Somewhere under the palace, there's a vault, a treasure room. Money. Gold. Jewels. That's what she cares about, her riches, not her human pet."

I paused, intrigued.

He reached out, putting his hands on the edge of the car. "I figure you probably have the weapons to get it done. Blow her finances to bits."

It wasn't like I had any other plans, and this sounded enjoyable. "What do you get out of it?"

"I want to ride back with you. And then when you get your job done, during the distraction, I want to help some of the other slaves escape. We were family in there. That's where my family is. I can't just leave them." He looked me in the eye, his gaze steady and unwavering.

He wanted to break the other slaves out. I paused for a long moment, letting him sweat as I pondered his words.

"Fine. But only because I'm bored."

~

Leon unwrapped the bandaging from his hand as he leaned against the TerrieV, the castles looming in the distance. "No infection. Is this how all the treatment in NewAmerica is?"

I stepped to the back, checking to be sure the med kit was ready, just in case anything went wrong. "Actually, MiraSalv is older. My parents invented it. My company is working on a newer, better version." I glanced over at him. "Will your arm slow our plan down?"

He shook his head as he traced the scabbed wound. "I go in, wait for you to bomb the vaults, and convince the slaves to leave with me. None of that requires difficult arm work."

"Things could go wrong. You might need to improvise."

"Koren and Ceba are hunting for us across the desert, and Stroben will be very preoccupied. Anyone else we meet will be much easier to work around. I mean, you're the Freedom Dreamer. Everyone in there either worships you or is terrified of you." He tore a new bandage, wrapping it around his arm. One handed, he tried twisting the gauze by his wrist, but it slid out of place.

"I'm not." I stepped over, reaching for the wrapping, gripping his arm as I bound it. "Are you sure you don't want a weapon?"

He shook his head as I finished the binding. "Stroben always has a weapon handy. I don't want to be like her."

"Fair enough." I grabbed a theta grenade out of the vehicle. "let's do this. When you're finished, bring the slaves to the new transport. We'll head for NewIstanbul and let them off there." It crossed my mind that we might be caught, even die. But whatever. It was Leon's plan, not mine.

He caught my hand as I turned away. "Thank you."

I glanced over to him before slowly pulling my hand away. "If anything funny happens, I'll leave without you," I didn't want him to mistakenly believe that I had formed some sort of attachment to him. I didn't attach myself to anyone. Not anymore. No one could replace Nessa.

"Yeah," he said slowly, but in his voice, I could hear the truth. He didn't think I would leave him. He thought I would wait for him. He thought I was one of the good guys. He was wrong.

Out of the Frying Pan

Dressed as a diplomat from the World Authority Association, wearing a rich, red and yellow dress, I was the sort of person who would not walk in step with someone as low as a food worker.

But here, at the base, under the shadow of the burning tree, standing amid the people who huddled around the dark castle, was where we were to part ways. I would simply step into Stroben's Castle, as a person of my status and power, a governmental worker, would need no invitation. No one from the World Authority Association asked permission.

Leon had the look of a basic lowlife, his only problematic feature his obvious slave tattoos. Even so, he'd be able to walk in without many questions. He wasn't someone who would be noticed around the cleaning areas or slave quarters.

He paused for a long moment. "You know where you're going?" He didn't dare turn to me, his voice was barely a whisper, his eyes locked on the huge black walls.

"Yes. You'll be fine waiting in the training rooms?" I watched as he fiddled with the edge of his shirt, his skin white. "Having second thoughts?"

He bit his bottom lip. "No. I'm not. I just—I'm not going to run into her. She won't even know I came back, not until we're gone."

"That's the plan, yes." I took a few steps past him, heading in the direction of the main gate. "I'll see you at the transport. I parked it outside of the kitchen entrance. You should see it as you head in. You've got twenty minutes after the blast, no more than that."

I assumed he nodded, but I heard nothing more than the slight scraping of his feet as he headed in his direction, losing himself to the crowd.

I entered, passing by guards and slaves with ease, slipping past those same expensive paintings and displays, heading for the lower floors. Down here, amid the slave quarters and the guardrooms, I would pass by unnoticed once more, as it would just be assumed that I required a slave for one reason or another.

A smile crept onto my lips. Reaching into my belt, I put my hand on the explosive device. This blast would ruin the integrity of the lower level, at the least, but it probably wouldn't collapse anything. It could also ruin the dining area above us, and break apart Leon's old room. It would take the financial vault down with it. Stroben's livelihood would crash into dust, robbing her of everything she ever loved. She would be brought to her knees. This would—

I froze. If this was truly where Stroben kept her treasure, wouldn't she have guards? Or cameras? Or at least a reinforced door to protect what was hers? Wouldn't it look less like a hole in the wall, and more like a vault? Wouldn't it look less like a cleaning closet? And to put this on a level of the building that only held slaves?

She was crazy, yes, but she was not an idiot. I stared at the door, at its unornamented, unsecured, pathetic frame. I'd simply taken Leon at his word, assuming that he'd blindly tell me the truth. But instead of leading me to a place that would dissolve Stroben's livelihood, he sent me to an area that could be destroyed without a single fatality, while creating enough chaos for him to get his friends out.

The worthless skunk didn't care if I got back at Stroben. He just told me what he knew I wanted to hear. He lied to me. And I'd just trusted him.

I reached out a cold hand, touching the handle of the door, pushing it open with a swift movement. The inner room illuminated.

It was nothing more than storage, boxes after boxes, items that had been cataloged, packed into something that was smaller than even the slave rooms were. Rage tinted my eyesight red as I stepped to the nearest crate, breaking it open. Under straw and packing material, I found the *treasure* that Leon had pointed me to. But it was a plaque with a NewAmerican seal of a tree, a token between her and some other company, a display from a lab she'd partnered with in NewAmerica. In fact, it looked like the MiraCorp symbol.

This trinket was here, this worthless monument. There were no jewels, no blocks of gold. There was not a single stack of UVs. There was nothing of value. A rage boiled through me, and I considered bombing the room anyway, just because I was annoyed.

But the object of my anger was not this room, not at all. It was that cowardly liar. I headed to the training area. I had to find Leon.

In the drill rooms, I slipped between four grey walls, all lined with various weapons. The sides of the room were padded, a brown color, and there was a soft mat on the floor. But he wasn't there. Over in a corner, there was a punching bag, weights, jump-ropes, extra mats. But no human. Along the back wall, there were sparring robes and chalk. But not a soul around.

Did he slink back to Stroben, like a dog begging his master to take him back? Or had he been caught as he'd waited for the commotion? How far did his deception go? And why did it sting like this?

I had to know. I had to hunt him down, I had to come up with a way to morph myself once more. Unless I found out otherwise, I had to assume that he had given Stroben every detail, including his knowledge of my disguise.

I turned the corner, a plan of attack not yet formed. I came to a grinding halt, almost slamming into a small slave.

She was shorter, young, with blond hair pulled tight behind her, done up into a bun. Her blue eyes were brought out by the slave tattoo. Her small figure was clad in a blue serving toga, leaving a shoulder bare.

The woman blinked back at me, taking me in as well. "Luna Storm?" She asked in a NewSerens accent, her voice small, and her adoration obvious. "You came back, eh?"

"You'll forget you saw me here," I ordered, wishing I could add a name to her face. "Irene."

She nodded. "Of course. I owe it to you."

I lifted a brow. "You... what?"

"You saved me."

These people were far too desperate for a savior. "I didn't save anyone. All I did was steal a slave from Stroben."

She shook her head. "I saw you. You dropped the medicine that Virginia used to save my life." She shrugged her shoulders. "She said Leon did it. But that weren't right, eh? You were the one."

I did drop the medicine, but that was the full extent of my actions. It wasn't to save her.

But that didn't mean I couldn't use this opportunity. "I need a change of clothes, something that will make me blend in."

"Anything for you." She nodded once. "This way." She gestured down the hallways, to the slave quarters. We passed few beings on the way, slaves who stared at me in adoration. Irene waved them away, pulling me into the hovel she called home.

I stepped into a single room, a single mat on the floor, as she pulled a crate out of the corner. She drew out clothing from what little she had. She tossed them to me. "I'll step out while you change." She moved to the hallway.

After throwing on the new outfit, I glanced at Irene's small mirror and I smiled. I was now dressed in a threadbare wool shirt, a size too small for me, black pants with a hole in them. I still wore the same black boots, but even with that defining mark, it looked good enough to get by. And with the fake slave markings now across my nose, ink marks, I'd fit in perfectly.

I saw a nobody, a woman who would be lost in the crowd. I saw her stand alone in a blank room with blank walls, empty, worthless, meaningless. The door was scuffed. The floor had never been cleaned. The simple mattress in one corner was torn and stained. I looked as if I fit right in with this environment. I had transformed. I stepped out.

"Thank you," I whispered. She'd given me the little she had.

Not that it mattered. It shouldn't matter. It didn't matter. I wasn't the sort of person who would let that matter.

"Anything I can do for the Freedom Dreamer."

I pursed my lips, aware of the fictional version of me that she was seeing. "I have to go," I had to find Leon and the truth, and then I had to vanish from this place forever. But this girl… she knew Leon. Maybe she had more that could be useful to me. "Do you know where he is?"

Her small smile faltered. "You come to save him again? I'm not sure you can get him out of this one, not after they caught him."

My throat closed in on itself. He hadn't betrayed me. He'd gotten caught. I swallowed my guilt. "What happened?"

She bowed her head. "There was a commotion. Koren was training, working on his hand to hand, but he was using one of us for practice. He's done it more than once, and the slaves don't always live through it." She wrapped her arms in front of her chest, huddling. "But then the Favored One swooped down, out of nowhere, like an angel, I heard. He got in Koren's way. But then the slave catcher sort of lost it. I could hear the screams from my quarters. I didn't even know a person could be hurt that badly. He didn't stop until Stroben herself came in."

"Is he in the med bay now?"

She shook her head. "Ceba brought him to the reformation cells."

"Ceba's here, too?"

"Yes. She and Koren, both."

Leon didn't back out on me, even if he'd lied. Perhaps he'd only been guilty of aiming for the least loss of life. And he'd stopped a slave from being beaten to death. If I didn't attempt to save a man like that, I'd dishonor the spirit of Nessa. Worse, I felt a burning feeling in my own gut. I wanted to save him. I wanted him back. I wanted him around.

"Where are the reformation cells?"

Into the Fire

I bolted to the security areas, my fake slave tattoos making me invisible to those I passed. Here was the first person who'd known me since Nessa, and he could be dying. I couldn't let that happen.

The entrance to the security area was closed, a security man standing before me. I skidded to a stop, attempting to look like I belonged here.

He lifted an eyebrow at me.

"Koren sent for me." I lied, realizing my own stupidity. This was never going to work.

"Koren doesn't send for anyone," He snorted, his blond hair falling into his eyes. "Run away, girl. You don't know what you're getting yourself into."

"No, Koren—

"Stop wasting my time. You're an idiot, trying to lie to me." He grabbed my shirt. "They're interrogating a slave in there, beating him within an inch of his life. And his only crime is that he was with the Freedom Dreamer. You—" His jaw slackened. "You're her."

I pulled away, but his grip tightened, holding me in place. "I don't know what you're talking about."

His eyes darkened. "Lies. Again. You're her, the one who dropped the med kid for Ire—for the slave."

I shook my head, pulling away again. "You are confused."

His brow lowered. "Why are you here? Dreamer, you're in the wrong sector. If you think we're bad, go to NewAmerica. They need you more there. They need a miracle, not us." After a long moment, he let go of my shoulder. "I'll tell them all you overpowered me. Now do what you came to do."

I stepped away from him, out of reach. "You're going to just… let me go?" He was going to just let me in? This was too easy.

"Yes. I'll make it look like you overpowered me. I'll tell Koren you came out of nowhere, then led me off on a chase. I'll cover for you as long as I can. You'll have all the time you need."

"Why are you doing this?" I folded my arms.

He took out his laser, emptying the electro-cartridge. "One of the slaves means something to me. I—" His jaw froze for a moment, shaping words that were new to his lips. "I care for her. I know I shouldn't. She's a slave. She should be nothing to any free man. But she's my world."

"They'll kill you if they find out you helped me." It wasn't going to sway his decision, but I felt like he had a right to know. "At least tell me your name."

"It's York." He shook his head. "I'll hack the cameras, so I won't get caught. If I do it right, I'll be disciplined, but I'll live." He nodded at me, and pulled away, swinging the door wide. I slid by.

I strode down the interrogation block, past dark rooms. I had been hoping for a simple extraction, but it sounded like I would have to wait my turn to enter his cell. I could hear Koren and Ceba at the far end of the detainment unit, even as I stood at the entrance. As sound came only from one room, that alcove at the end of the path, tucked away. Only there, there were scuffs and movement and ragged breathing.

Passing through the shadows of the hallway, I peered past the bars, into the commotion that was unfolding. Behind a backdrop of the crest, I saw the silhouette of a towering Stroben, her fists against her hips. She stood opposite a half-naked Leon, who had morphed into a pathetic mess. He was bound to the chair, cowering, shaking, sweat dripping down his face. Behind the Brokel, one on each side, stood two beings, one with knives and lasers and cuffs decorating her belt and arms, the other seemingly weaponless.

"—me, master." Leon coughed out. "I would never betray you." He swallowed, looking up at her once more, with tearstained eyes that reflected the white lights. "You own me." My chest burned as I heard the honesty in his tone.

Ceba snorted. "Finally. The first truth you've given us." She turned to Stroben. "I'll start with some more Deprov, and then the fun—

Stroben held up a hand to cut her off. "I don't want to know, just do it. When he's done, bring him to me. I will make sure he remembers his place."

She turned on her heel, heading to the hallway, passing by without noticing my figure in the darkness. With her steps echoing down the dark path, Koren and Ceba were left alone with the slave.

Ceba reached out, grabbing Leon by his hair to force him into looking at her. "Looks like Stroben isn't here to protect you." She wasted no time in drawing a knife, complete with dried blood. "Now it's our turn." I grit my teeth, waiting for my opportunity. I couldn't step in, not with both Koren and Ceba there. I had to wait.

"No marks," Koren hissed, pulling her back. "Not for the precious Favored One. Let me take care of this."

He turned. Standing in front of Leon, he looked over the chattel.

Leon held his gaze for mere seconds before his eyes fell once more.

"Oh, no, no, no, you pathetic little princess, don't be scared. I want you to…" he stepped to the corner of the room, grabbing another chair, "feel as if we're friends. Brothers, even." He slammed the seat across from Leon's, sitting backwards, placing his hand on the slave's bare leg. "Don't you want to be brothers?"

Leon blanched. "We are not—"

"Brothers," Koren insisted. "Just like Believers of Love. They always call each other a Brother or a Sister. Like your old girlfriend. What was her name again?"

Leon gagged.

"Use your words, Favored One. You know how it gets when you try to break my rules."

He shook his head, biting his lip, tears flowing down his face.

"Words," Koren spat, backhanding Leon across the face.

"Echo," Leon's voice broke. "My Echo."

I stepped forward, barely able to keep myself back as I watched my companion. But with a wave of willpower, I held myself back. I was no match for the two slavecatchers in their own territory.

"Echo." Koren let the word hang in the air. "That girl you got killed. So, it's like *you* killed her, isn't it? You were the one who laced that drink. You were the one who tried to poison Stroben. You were the one who even admitted to it, verified that it was poisoned. And you were the one who could do nothing but watch as they poured your own poison down Echo's throat. Now the only thing left of her is…" He drew out a pendant of some sort, a—

Her Medallion. I gritted my teeth against the pain in my chest, knowing I couldn't act yet.

Seeing it, Leon shriveled, a single sob slipping through his lips. The slavecatcher gave a small laugh. "I thought so. I found it in your clothes."

I reached for Nessa's Believer Medallion, clinging to it with white knuckles.

Leon shook his head, pulling his chin in as he stared at the floor. "It's not hers," he coughed out.

"Oh," Koren said as Ceba handed him a small lighter. "But it is." He flicked his fingers, and a small flame glimmered in the darkness.

The light reflected across Leon's cheeks, illuminating tear stains. Koren lifted the wooden chip above the flame.

Leon sniveled, watching the action. "It's all I have left of her, Koren. Please." His head dropped. "I'll do anything."

Ceba snickered, stepping in, running her hands through the slave's hair, making it stand up. "Oh, you pathetic slave," she offered, "I know you will."

Koren put the flame under the wooden medallion, letting the fire do its work.

There were more words to be said, but Leon had broken. There was little more for me to do, except to wait them out, however long it would take. I curled into the corner, covering my ears with my hands, burying my head in my knees, shrouded by the shadows.

I knew the darkness of dusk claimed the world outside, though it would be impossible to tell the difference between day and night in the prison. It was designed, as the time turned, for Leon to have no concept of how long he'd been there.

But I knew. Three hours. He'd been interrogated for the first hour, and the rest was just time to let the drug wear off. They left, but within minutes, Koren and Ceba would be coming back to clean him up and transport him to Stroben.

But for now, Leon needed no supervision. I had no idea how debilitating the drug was, yet here he was, unable to think clearly enough to get himself to the door. And it wasn't even locked anymore.

Uncovering my ears, stepping out of the shadows, towards his alcove, I finally spoke. "This wasn't part of our plan, Slave."

90

He glanced up with glassy eyes. He struggled, attempting to form his thoughts together into words. "They never let me wear a shirt." It was the first time in hours he'd been able to speak a full sentence.

My chest burning for him, I reached my sleeve out, wiping the sweat and tears off his cheek, over the tattoo. I reached down, checking his pulse. "A shirt?"

He didn't react to my motions. I wasn't sure he even knew I was there. "One shirt. Just one." He gave a hysterical laugh. "I shouldn't care. She can dress her pets however she wants."

I crouched in front of him, taking in his swimming, glassy, red eyes. "Leon, why did you tell me to blow up the storeroom?"

He snorted, his fingertips shaking. "The storeroom?" He shrugged his shoulder painfully. "I was scared she'd hurt someone. She hurt me. What if she's like just Stroben?"

"Shandra just wanted to find her friend. Stroben is a warlord."

He gave a weak snort. "She attacked me. She broke my nose." He pulled against the restraints at his legs. "Where am I?"

I didn't picture Leon to be the obviously ungrateful sort. "Shandra helped you escape."

"A glitch." A bead of sweat dripped down his face. "I wanted her to be different. There was a second, when I was working with the car, when she was like Echo." His voiced cracked again. "But they both hurt me. Stroben was right. She's not a Freedom Dreamer. She's just another warlord."

My temper flared. "Shandra was not like Stroben." I was done arguing with him. He was a slave. He was nothing. His opinion did not matter. "You spew lies again, and I'll shut your mouth for you."

He gagged. "Master." His demeanor changed from a chaotic drug-ridden stature to pure terror. "Master, I didn't realize—" He slammed his jaw closed.

I blinked at him. Stroben and I really were one. We were powerful and corrupt. We were exact reflections of one another. We were villains.

But I really wanted Leon to think we were different. "Listen. I don't know if you'll remember this after the drugs wear off, but I'm going to say it anyway. As of this moment, Stroben and I are no longer the same, because she enslaves you, and I am going to set you free."

I would not be the villain of my own story.

Improv

Leon had to get out of this building. I needed a distraction. An explosive distraction, something that would make the escape of the Favored One a minor event.

I had to blow up the storeroom, which meant I had to leave Leon, and pick him up later. My skin burned at the thought of leaving him alone when his interrogators could come back at any moment, but I didn't see another way. As for the rest of his slave friends, I didn't care about them. But he did. And I had to convince him that I wasn't like Stroben.

I stepped away, out into the hallway, toward the slave quarters. I didn't have to be silent anymore, didn't need to hide. I had to focus, take whatever step was next, but Leon's screams, from hours ago, still echoed in my brain. His sobs, now a memory, struck me, knocking the wind from me. His bruising stung my core.

I moved to Irene's hovel, striding in, the dust irritating my eyes, dripping tears down my face.

"Dreamer," she said, rising in the darkness. "Is he alive?"

I covered my mouth, trying to cover the pain, but instead, my vision tinted red once more. "He's fine. But I can't do this alone." I cut myself off, waiting out the wave of emotion that struck me again. When I spoke again, my voice was strong. "Gather whatever slaves you can find and bring them to the transport by the kitchen entrance. I will meet you there soon."

She nodded. "It will be done. Will you be okay?"

I shook my head, waving her away. I had to bomb the building. And I had to get back to Leon.

Sweat lining my palms, I moved down the hallways, to the blank door to the closet, grenade in hand.

In a swift action, I pulled the pin on the bomb, launching it at the door, turning on my heel. I changed the settings on the bomb from three minutes to a much shorter time, knowing that every moment wasted was a moment in which Leon suffered.

One. I turned, heading down the hallway, my vision tunneling, hearing the dramatic click as my foot hit the ground.

Two. I took in a single, ragged breath. I was closer to safety, but I wasn't far enough.

Three. I felt salt on my upper lip as I sucked in another breath of air.

Four. I flew up one step, another, with burning energy.

Five. First landing. Here, then gone.

Six. Almost ther—

It struck, slamming me to the ground as the world tore itself apart, cracks dancing on the walls, dust and debris pouring into the air. The stone steps beneath me shook with the power of the blast, shaken by the disaster I had caused. But, just as Leon planned, the destruction was largely of objects, and not of humans. It was something Nessa would have appreciated.

I let relief flood through me. It wasn't as if I foresaw myself being injured by my own action, but the fact that it was over, and I was unharmed was energizing. I'd pulled this part of the plan off. I turned away, moving to the Brokel's quarters. By now, Leon was probably there.

The doors to Stroben's personal quarters were slightly ajar. She'd left in a hurry, a good sign. If the woman herself and her bodyguards weren't there, it would be easier to get Leon.

As I stepped in, I entered a new world. It was large, decorated, rich, a dramatic change from the thin, blank hallways outside. It had a kitchen through one hallway that looked like my own, out in NewAmerica. I turned away, glancing to the electronic center with an imaging device, as well as a communicator, neither illuminated. Then, finally, past the entry area, there was the bedroom. Leon had to be there.

And there, curled in a corner, a leash tying him to the wall, was Leon. He was curled among thin sheets and bare pillows on the floor, a bed for an animal. His blank, oblivious expression cut into my chest. "Leon," I whispered, trying not to break him further. "We have to go."

Alone in the dark, he swallowed once, his face bruised from the interrogation. "She's going to hurt them."

"What?" Now was not the time for this.

"Any protection we have, anything, it all comes from her." He choked. "And now she hates me, so she's going to hurt them. Virginia. Johal. Irene. Arron. All of them."

His features had given up on any semblance of sane thought. Whatever his interaction with Stroben had been, it left him worse than the interrogation.

"She's upset with me." He blinked at the wall. "And she knows they're my family. This is my fault. Every cut. Every scream. All of it. I should have thought of this before I ran. I should have known Stroben would take away their protection."

I stepped into his line of vision, turning his jaw to me. I stared at him, at his bright eyes, dim with Deprov, at his perfectly clipped hair that was meant to be messy and sloppy, at his empty expression. I crouched next to his sheets as I worked at his leash, untying him. "Leon. Listen to me. You don't need Stroben to protect you. I will protect you. And if that fails, Leon, you will learn to protect yourself." I grabbed his hand. "But if you want to escape with the other slaves, we have to leave right now."

He blinked, dragged back into reality. "They're escaping?" his voice sounded thick. His shoulders straightened, the fog leaving his expression.

I nodded. "But we need to go right now."

He stood, his legs shaking. I gripped his arm, keeping him steady. After a long moment, he took a step forward, then another. "I can do this," he whispered, pulling away from me. "I can walk by myself."

96

Glancing over his wounds, I nodded hesitantly. This might give him back control that had been robbed from him. We moved out of the room, down the hallway.

"Shandra. How did you find me?" His voice raw from the interrogation, he stumbled, his head down. "After Koren attacked me, I was sure you'd run."

"Running is something Stroben would do. And I'm not like her." Even if I did hurt people,

He laughed weakly, unnerved. "I never said you two were—

"Slave," a voice cut in, from down the hall, one that belonged to power and authority and insanity. "What are you doing out of the chambers?"

She was standing in the doorway, wearing a shocked expression, halfway down the steps, a security man gesturing to the wall as her fingertips traced a large crack. Her expression was furious, distracted by a million other problems. But as she locked eyes, her look sharpened, finally finding an outlet for her rage. But her being here was an outlet for my rage as well.

Leon froze in his tracks, staring at his master through the dusty air. I grabbed at him, pulling him forward. "He's leaving," I spat.

Stroben, crossing her arms, glanced over my thin shirt and worn pants. Her eyes moved back to Leon. "Get back to where I left you."

He drew back, standing behind me as he mumbled something indistinguishable. After a moment, he bit his lip, wrapping his arms around himself as his skin turned shock white.

"Excuse me?" Stroben put her hand on her belt, by her gun, her features darkening.

"No." He whispered, shaking his head this time. "I said—" His voice broke, and I stepped in front of him. "I just—"

"Shut your mouth," She demanded, and his jaw slammed closed. "You ungrateful beast. Go back, this instant, or I will call Koren."

"Do it. I don't care." His admission halted both me and Stroben. "I don't care."

There was a silent moment, filled with Stroben's rage, anger at the state of her building, fury at finding her slave out of his den, wrath at his insurgence. She lifted her wrist to her lips. "Koren. The Favored One is acting up. Show him his place. And maybe collect a few of his friends. You know how much he likes that." Koren said something indistinguishable on the other end. "Excellent." Her lips formed a grin as she looked at Leon. "We'll be seeing you soon." She shut off her communicator.

Leon stared back at her in silence as I calculated how many weapons I had, and if I could take her and Koren alone.

"Or," she hissed, stepping to the side, drawing out a hilted whip, "We could end this, now. I'm not sure I like you all prettied up. Perhaps this rule against scarring is where this rebellion is coming from." Snakelike, she lashed out around me, striking him.

Leon took the blow to the face and neck, blood instantly marking his skin. He gasped, pressing his hand to the side of his face, a look of shock and pain across his features.

I stepped forward. "I'm taking your slave away," I hissed. "And I'm getting your claws off of him."

Her eyes glowed with energy. "Storm. I almost didn't recognize you. How nice of you to come back. It makes tracking you so much easier."

"It's Shandra, actually," I spat. "And don't thank me. Destroying your universe was the least I could do."

Snarling, she dealt another blow, this time at me. I stepped forward, catching the whip with my arm, watching as it wrapped its teeth around my skin, shocked at the pain that enveloped my arm. Leon had taken it without a word, but I was screaming on the inside.

I yanked the tool out of Stroben's hand's, pulling it to me. "He hates you." My voice was tight with pain. "You treat him like he's worthless. But he's not an animal. He's a human, and no one can own him." A support under the hallway crumbled, shaking the room as I gripped the whip, snapping it at her. It struck her forearm, leaving a line of red.

Leon choked in horror. I was shocked, too. Running was becoming a great option.

Stroben stared at me for a long moment, almost not understanding. As beads of blood appeared, she sharpened her expression. "You dare strike a

Brokel. I'll have to do this slowly." She drew out a jagged knife.

As she took a step forward, the ceiling between us crumbled, leaving boulders to fall from above. Someone had shot a laser at the weakened structure. As the rocks fell, I saw the figure of the guard, York, diving through the rubble at us.

He was struck by a stone, leaving a jarring mark of blood down his left arm. "She is not going to take that well," he said through clenched teeth. "Maybe we should think about fleeing. You know, in terror and all that."

Hamartia of the Heart

Leon ran with me, his expression pained as blood dribbled down the side of his face. "Shandra, you attacked a Brokel."

I nodded as we turned to the exit. "Yep." I took a deep breath. "I was there."

"No. You don't understand. Attacking a Brokel is punishable by death." He sucked in air for a moment. "She'll hunt you down and murder you. In fact, she'll probably make me do it."

I snorted. "I would like to see you try. Or her, for that matter."

York laughed, a sound clipped by his pain.

"And for any of that to happen, she'd have to catch us, first." Grimacing, I left the building, bolting into the night, coming to the transporter, a plane-like leisure craft. I ran past the slaves. Apparently, Irene was successful in convincing the others to follow her. There were about thirty people on board, waiting for us. At least that part of the plan went well.

We stepped into the cockpit and Leon continued. "You don't get it. She'll let you think you've gotten away. She'll let us run, let the other slaves go, let you finally hope that you're safe. And that's when she'll catch you. She will snag you and bring you back."

I sat in the pilot's seat, plugging numbers into the controls. His words weren't helping my focus. "Once again, I'm not worried. Even if everything falls apart, we both get caught, and she pits you against me, it's fine. I'd crush you."

"Shandra. This isn't a joke. I've seen her do this before."

I pulled out, flying away from the castle, gritting my teeth in annoyance. "I know. But she was hurting you. I had a chance to stop her, and I don't regret it."

He turned forward, taking in the night sky before us. "Not yet, you don't."

Or did I? I'd traded Leon's life for mine. Away from the heat of the moment, I wondered if it was worth it. He was a slave, and I was practically a queen. Wasn't his life worth less? Had I made the right choice?

Standing, I set the transport to autopilot, heading to NewIstanbul. There, I would let the slaves begin their new lives. If I just sold them again, they'd fall back into Stroben's hands easily. At least this way, they'd be significantly harder for her to collect.

I drew out of the cockpit, to the main area of the ship. I passed slaves as they attempted to hide their tattoos, leaving their faces smudged with black streaks and bleached with discolored cover-up. Where they got the makeup, I hadn't a clue. After seeing the grinning faces, I broke out the bar at the front of the transport, and the meals, more importantly the drinks, were on the house. This celebration may have been a bit premature, what with Ceba and Koren looking for us. But life was short, and the bar was full.

Irene, her tattoo shaded into a deep blue strip across her face, stood by the bar, York beside her. She laughed at something he said, her eyes alight with a soft energy. He reached out, catching her hand. He pressed his lips to his knuckles, and she blushed happily.

I looked at my own fingers, remembering when Leon held my hand, thanking me.

I grabbed another pint, looking through the crowd for him. He was sitting in the corner, alone, his shoulders sharp, his eyes too focused to have been anything but sober. He looked back at me with a critical expression on his bruised face.

I shook my head. He probably thought I was an idiot, celebrating right now. Or maybe he was too brutalized from the interrogation to smile. Or maybe he was just thoughtful rather than celebratory. Or maybe, he was looking at the Freedom Dreamer, the woman who rescued him, the NewAmerican who fought for every slave. Maybe he thought I was a hero. And if he thought it, maybe I could be.

Maybe he didn't want to look at me. I took a swallow of alcohol. Maybe he saw the monster I was, my own greed and rage. I drank again. Maybe he thought I was like Stroben, a violent giant. I gulped down the rest of my drink, reaching for another. Maybe he remembered what if felt like when I broke his nose.

I drank deeply. Maybe, just for tonight, I could forget.

Discoveries

The bite from the whip burned the side of my face, made tenfold by the hammering headache I had. When I opened the door to the city, letting in the desert sunlight, I was hit with nausea. The ramp slid out, allowing for transportation to the ground, and I flinched at the sound.

York was dressed in clothing from the Serens, something that would make him easily blend into the strange culture of NewIstanbul. He, like the others, would return to a long-forgotten family, or to a new life. Although, with York specifically, I suspected Irene was in his future. But either way, all the slaves would be painfully hard for Stroben to track. At least I wouldn't be the only power-hungry loser who was miserable.

They were beginning to file out, walking past me. And there, halfway through the pack, was him. Leon. He didn't seem hungover, at least not as badly as the other revelers, but he seemed miserable on a deeper level. I wondered if his nose hurt.

"Off to the Serens, then?" he asked tentatively.

"Is that where you want to go? Or do you have some other place in mind?" I should have been over it, but I really wanted him to stay.

Tracing the whip marks on his face as he looked at mine, he paused for a long moment. "You came back."

"You would have done the same." I shrugged. "It was nothing." It wasn't easy to save him, and I still wasn't sure trading his life, only to get a price on my head, was a good call. And I didn't even get a thank you kiss. But that wasn't what I was supposed to say.

"I would be back there, like that, if you hadn't helped me. Again." He glanced up, sincerity in his eyes. "You rescued them. And you saved me."

If I was going to pretend it was easy, I was going to have to go the whole way. "You were caught because you fought Koren. I heard you saved some slave's life back there. How could I leave a man like that to die?" Nessa would never forgive me.

"I helped one slave, and he might not even have died. You saved them all." He drew himself up. "That's what a Freedom Dreamer does. I want to be right there, beside you, working with you."

"You want to work with me?" I was reminded of when he left the first time, in NewIstanbul. Here he was, offering to stay with me again. A wave of energy flowed through me at the thought of having a partner. But... "I'm not planning any great escapes. There's not really a team, here. and I'm not really a Freedom Dreamer."

He gave a soft smile. "I'd be okay with normal life, too. As long as I was with you."

"Fine, then." But only because I was having a generous day.

Leon stood beside me as the last few slaves filed out, slipping into the masses, losing themselves to the throngs. Only a few were left, still by the ship, Irene among them. She stood, holding the hand of the guard, York. He whispered something to her, and she giggled, laughing back at him.

She stood close to the ship, her tattoo markings dark in the shade as she waited for me to notice her. This couldn't be good. "Irene?"

She took a step forward, her figure lit by the bright sunlight, York behind her. "I wanted to thank you for what you did."

"You helped. You got the others out while I found Leon." And she didn't have to narrowly escape the Brokel, so she honestly did better than I did.

"But it would have been impossible without you, eh? I, we," she gestured to York. "We wanted to thank you. I'd like to give you something meaningful."

Nothing mattered to me. I was heartless and proud of it. Wasn't I?

"Leon said you were searching for a Believer who had disappeared." York spoke this time, his voice soft.

"What?" Nessa?

They stepped into the shade of the transport, and their figure went dark. "There are slaves being sold in NewAmerica as test subjects." York lowered his head. "I know because I was there for the deals. Sometimes, they need security personal for slave shipments, part of Stroben's enterprises." His eyes unfocused, caught in a miserable memory. "Often, I was chosen. The slaves I worked with tended not to die on route, so Stroben would turn a blind eye if

106

I let one or two go missing. Your friend could have been sold overseas, like the others."

I shook my head. I had no time for this. "NewAmerica is a free country. They don't buy slaves there. Trust me, Nessa is dead. I have her medallion."

"There are slaves there," Irene cut in. "My brother is there. He moved to NewAmerica, to get enough UVs to buy me from Stroben. He worked on a ranch, I think. He was caught and York found him in the facility. They—I got letters, for a while. York smuggled them through, but there is no way anyone, not even someone as strong as my brother, could stay alive this long. Not in the Green Tree of MiraCorp."

For a moment, I thought she'd said MiraCorp. But there was nothing wrong with my company. They cut me huge checks and I let them do their thing. But kidnapping was not their thing. They created medicines, not widows. She must have been wrong. She had to be.

"You can believe me, or not," She shook her head. "But what other leads do you have?"

"I have her medallion." I yanked it out. She had to understand that she was wrong. My company was not evil. "Do you need more proof than that?" Their presence was increasingly aggravating. This slave and her boyfriend did not have the right to talk to me.

Silently, with a meaningful glance to Leon, Irene stepped away. As they walked, York wrapped his arms around her, and they stepped into the sunlight and a second chance at life.

And I turned to Leon. "You told them I was looking for Nessa? Do you enjoy getting under my skin?" My hands bunched into fists as I grit my teeth.

He pulled out the chain that used to hold Echo's medallion, as if his girlfriend's necklace would convince me. "They burned it while I was in the detainment room. It was all I had left of her, and they stole it from me."

"I do not care about your—

"They burned it."

I froze. Nessa was sent to the afterlife in a funeral pyre, and the wooden trinket made it through? I drew out the perfectly intact, unburned token.

"How well do you know your company?"

Part III War at Home

Unbroken

I put my hand on the navigator, adjusting the coordinates into the digital screen. After a moment, my face still stinging, I fell back into a leather seat. I looked out, staring at the waves of sand, each one sparkling with sunlight, glinting as we passed by.

I brought my knees up to my chin, watching as the day slowly waned, opening to a soft dusk, allowing stars to accent the darkness. With their twinkling came a terrible hope in my heart. I let myself grasp for straws I'd sworn to avoid. My chest burned. Why did it feel like this? This medallion should have burned with her, but it didn't. The story of her death was flawed. Was it real? If not, was MiraCorp the place to begin to look? My company was beyond reproach. It was, after all, mine. But wasn't it as good a place as any to pick up my search? Or should I turn around, go back to Stroben's palace? No. I had to show the world that MiraCorp was—

"Can I know what you're thinking?" Leon's voice cut through the silence, bouncing at me from the doorway.

Crinkling my nose, wincing as the movement stung my cuts, I glanced to him, taking in his quiet figure.

How had he been able to sneak up like that? I mentally reminded myself to buy a lock.

He rubbed his hands together. "I mean, you've been here for a while now, and I just wanted to know what your thoughts were?"

"You want to know my thoughts? For a slave, you're bold." But the moment the words left my lips, I regretted them. They were not what Leon needed to hear.

Leon backed into the hallway. "You're right. I'm sorry. I didn't mean to offend you." He bowed his head, blushing, whispering something to himself.

"No, no. Leon, get back here," I growled, annoyance bleeding through my tone.

He froze. "Yes, mas—" He swallowed, cutting his voice into silence as he walked back in, his limbs obeying robotically.

"No, that's not how I meant it. I just..." I was bad at this. I felt like companions were supposed to like... talk. About stuff. Like what was on their minds. But this was hard, after losing my friend. Becoming close to someone else felt like betraying her.

But having a friend again might be nice. "I was thinking about Nessa," I said, surprising myself. "I was..." Scared. "worried to hope that Nessa is alive. I feel in my heart that she is. But what if she's not, and I'm just setting myself up for failure?" Did I say too much?

He nodded, coming to the copilot's seat, bringing his knees to his chin. After a moment, he curled in on himself, mirroring me. "Yeah, hope can be like that. It's scary, sometimes."

I jerked to him, snarling. "I am not afraid." Instantly, I bit my tongue. How did people not lash out at their friends?

He glanced at me, exasperated, half smiling. "You know what I mean." He sat up, his posture sturdy and strong. His nose and arm wcre healed. Even the bruising from the interrogation was beginning to fade. I liked him like this.

"So, what's on your mind?" I was done sharing my life. It was his turn.

He laughed, a strange expression that showed his perfect teeth. "I... no. You don't want to know."

"I asked. I care about the answer." Well, I didn't really *care,* care. Now that he avoided the question, I was invested.

"You do?" He took a breath. "No. You don't. You think you do, but when I tell you, you'll wish you didn't. You'll correct me for it."

"I'll what?"

He shrugged. "You'll decrease food portions until I see the error in my thoughts. Or find some Koren-type guy to teach me." He paused for a long moment. "Or you'll just throw me away."

"Leon." He was being way too honest about his life, and I did not have enough practice being a friend to deal with this. "If someone does that, they should be shot." Or better yet, I could shoot them.

"You can tell me the truth. You have my word that I won't hurt you."

His expression screamed of his disbelief as he lifted an eyebrow. But, ever submissive, he worked his jaw open. "I was thinking about Stroben's palace." He gave a guilty glance to the floor.

I lifted my eyebrows at him.

He was toying with a string on his clothes. "I should just move on. I mean, she would hit me if she was having a bad day. She'd hurt people, just to watch my reaction to it. If I *stood up to her*, Koren and Ceba would work on me until I saw my mistake. I mean, Stroben owned me. I was nothing without her. And I miss the other slaves. I know I can't go with them. Stroben will look hardest for me."

"What?" That would have been nice to know before I took him on.

He shrugged. "I'm the Favored One. And I made her look bad. I'll be her biggest target. Well, me or you. If I went with the others, I'd put them at risk. So I can't be near them. But that doesn't mean I don't miss them."

"You're allowed to have feelings." Now, that was probably a great sentence for a friend to say.

"Don't get me wrong, at the palace, I was treated better than most. I mean, I was a Favored One. She'd let me sleep in her room, on a mat on the floor. She even let me get away with things. Like, she knew I was good with machines. As a Favored One, they had me chained up quite a lot, but their

112

equipment was old. I knew how to take the cuffs off. It was a basic spring and lock system. She caught me. I thought she was going to kill me, but she just said that I was a clever little Favored One. She didn't even tell Koren. She said it would be our secret, my newest trick. She looked at me like I wasn't worthless. I'm messed up, right? Missing all that?"

"It sounds like you're human, and you're confused." And damaged.

He answered with silence.

I took in the creases in his brow, wondering if it was okay for me to end the conversation now. Would a friend do that? "Time will help you move on. Other relationships, friends and whatnot, they'll help you, too."

"Friends. Good friends." He gulped. "Like you?" He bit his lip, waiting for my answer.

I wasn't the friend sort. And I was even less of the 'good friends' sort. I never could be like that. I was a bad person. But Leon was worth fighting for, and he listened when I spoke. He was someone I would like to be around more. What would Nessa want me to say? "Yes. Like me."

And as much as admitting to this annoyed me, the idea was beginning to grow on me.

What NewAmerica Holds

We walked through the streets of NewSeattle, striding by the various stores. "If you're going to show up to MiraCorp as my bodyguard, you're going need to look the part. Think of it this way. You'll finally own another shirt." I toyed with the taser on my hip. He was probably going to have to arm himself, too.

He lifted a brow. Evidently, he was too high to remember that rant of his. "I can't. I won't be able to pay you back." He gestured to the thin shirt he was wearing. "I can just wear this. I found it in the transport."

"No. That's plaid. You aren't wearing that." I stepped forward, pointing at a designer plated black top. "This is more like what you should wear."

His nose scrunched. "That?"

I nodded. "Or anything else around here you like. Anything that's not…" I gave a pointed look to his current outfit. "checkered."

"All of these stores have outfits I can pick from?" He looked around the plaza at the brands and advertisements.

"Well, not the food places. But any clothes store, yes."

"Can I pick it?" He stared at me, swallowing, suddenly nervous. "Or do you pick it for me?"

I tilted my head. Why would I—Oh. Stroben chose what he got to wear at the palace. "You get to pick. That's how it works in NewAmerica."

After three stores, he finally chose a tan, armored design. It had a hood on the top of it, one that looked like a lion's mane, but Leon defended the style to a fault. I'd never heard him laugh so much as he made his selection. I thought he would have looked dashing in the black armor, but it had pink lines on the sides. He said the coloring was insulting to his masculinity. It sounded like an excuse to me.

But Leon was entranced by nothing but his clothing. He was too happy to be bashful. It was innocent and refreshing. "It's legit. I haven't picked my own clothes in…" His voice sounded light. "You should punch me. I bet it won't even hurt."

"Is that so?"

"Yeah. They said the plates are bulletproof."

"But not punch proof. Also, the gaps between the plating might take a beating. Try not to bet your life—"

I paused, the hair on the back of my neck rising. Here we were, in broad daylight, walking through a sunlit street. The crowd surged around us, oblivious and innocent. We melted into our surroundings with our modern armor. No one had taken notice of us.

Leon's stride stuttered. "Koren?"

That name, in this setting, was impossible. Yet, there he was, loitering outside a NewAgeCafe. How was he here? How did they find me this fast? Was nowhere safe?

I was suddenly paralytically aware of Stroben's oath to hunt me. "Leon, we need to keep walking.

This is a crowded street, and he wouldn't do anything with this many witnesses." Right? They wouldn't try to kill me here?

He choked, clearly in disagreement. "Unless he just destroys everyone. Koren can murder every human within view, Shandra. He'll—"

Koren flung his arm out, gesturing us over.

Leon sputtered on the edge of panic. "Shandra?"

As he spoke, a red dot appeared on his chest. It was a target mark, aimed from above, from a rooftop overhead. Koren leered.

Leon glanced down to his chest, to the flicker of light that warned of his fragile lifespan. We were, apparently, going to have a conversation with Koren. I gritted my teeth, willing the fear away.

As we walked up, Koren laughed. "Closer." Leon edged nearer, continuing until Koren nodded, indicating that he was close enough, within arm's reach. Leon stared as if he was meeting a ghoul.

"Favored One." Koren's voice was aggravatingly friendly. "We were worried about you. And here you are, out shopping. Now, is that wise? I'd be so deeply crushed if you'd gotten hurt in NewAmerica, where Stroben can't protect you. Pets should know not to stray from their owners."

As I snarled at the hunter, Leon's fingertips shook against my hand. I hadn't even realized that they were interwoven. I opened my mouth, attempting an angry, unafraid tone. "What do you want?"

"Me? I don't want anything," Koren spat, watching the target dance across Leon's torso. "Stroben does. The Brokel seemed real unhinged when you left. Put a price on the head of your friend here, in case you didn't know. She's also got some great changes for you when you're returned. Want to hear about it?"

"Please, no," Leon whispered, a sound so small that it was almost inaudible. I drew closer to him, gripping his hand harder.

Koren snarled, continuing. "We've got this nasty closet that you're going to call home, and it's got a lock on it, so when you're bad, we can put you back in your box. You're going to be put on half rations. And Ceba and I are going to get the chance to whip you into shape. Literally. Ceba is excited about that one."

"You think I'll let you?" My voice rang with resolve and I put my hand on my belt, by my taser.

He snorted. "Oh. We'll take care of you before then."

"But—but Stroben doesn't like it when-when you mark me." Leon's voice trembled. "She'll protect me."

"Are you serious?" Koren laughed, still ignoring me. "Didn't you hear? Stroben's willing to pay for corrective surgeries now. Just wait until you see all the new tricks I have. I mean, after what we've got planned, you'll be begging to crawl to Stroben's feet again, if only because it's the one place where you can hide from me."

"I don't want to go back."

Koren reached out, caressing the tattoo across Leon's face. "Who said you had a choice?" Leon flinched away.

"I did." I drew out my taser rod, stabbing forward. My hand ran the tool into Koren's shoulder, sending a dazzling light through his arms and legs. As he shook, sparks snapping through the air, a shot rang out.

Leon fell backwards, onto the street, crumpling. With the sound of a gunshot, the crowd spun out of control. Rich shoppers in sleek, high collared jackets shrieked in terror, shoving past one another in the chaos. Men in tunics and armored vests sprinted by. Children in synthetic armor ducked for cover.

I looked back to my companion, sprawled on the sleek pavement. If Leon was still alive, maybe I could use my—

He reached out, panicked as he rose. He wrapped an arm around his chest, his eyes wide with adrenaline.

I stared at his sudden revival for only a moment, looking into his perfect hazel eyes, too grateful to question this twist of fate. Within moments, we dove down a side street, stepping into an alley I knew well. Flying through, we turned a corner onto a rundown pathway. The stained newspapers and trash in our path, the broken apartment sign, the old buildings, were signs I knew well, indicators of our incoming safety.

Within moments, I stepped up to our safehouse. Opening the door, I realized it was as she had left it. I'd been paying rent on the place, in case she wanted it back when I found her. No one had disturbed it.

My hand was still resting on the door handle, surprised that I had been the one to open it. She'd always let me in, before. By me, on a small table, there was her favorite mug. I picked it up, glancing at the black ink scrawled across it. I looked up to a chair in the corner, a blanket thrown over it. Her heating had been turned off once, so we'd shared the blanket as we talked for hours. I wasn't sure where, but I was sure she still had that dress I let her borrow for a celebration. All her things were here, but she wasn't. How could I still miss her this much?

"Where are we?" Leon asked as he took in the peeling paint and rotted walls, eyes glassy with pain. "Do Koren and Ceba know about this place?"

"They won't find us." I took in the stain by the door. "Nessa's apartment. Only she knew. Knows."

"No one but her? No one else? You never brought your boyfriend here or anything?"

"Um. No." Wow. He just had to make it awkward. But then, with the sweat pouring down his face, awkward was the least of his worries.

He leaned against the wall, slipping to a sitting position on the floor. I kneeled next to him, pulling apart his armor to inspect the injury. There wasn't any blood, which was a miracle, but the breastplate was dented.

"Bulletproof, right?" He was shaking, his teeth clenched.

I nodded. Already, there was a deep bluish mark covering his left torso, dancing over his skin like a painful kiss. With every breath, his chest shook.

I pressed softly on each rib to check for breakage. He locked his jaw, his skin whitening, but he didn't scream. They weren't broken. The fact he was still conscious meant that he didn't have severe internal bleeding. If the shock from the pain didn't kill him, the most serious problem was the growing bruise, from his neck to his hip. "You've very lucky," I mused.

He grit his teeth. "I don't feel lucky."

I nodded, too focused to say more as I pulled out a small med pack, tearing out what little IceCloth I had, strapping it to the wounded area. I wrapped the strips across his chest, pulling them tight to keep the bruising pressurized.

I pulled out the VitaK, injecting into his arm. "You know," he said, his eyes losing focus after the dose. "That was the moment. When the car broke." He took a long breath. "She was standing there, all clueless, her brown hair in her eyes as she pointed at the car. It was the first time I was strong, helpful. It was the first time she needed me. I think I—I care for her."

I taped down the white strips of cooling material. Did he just— This VitaK was apparently very hard

120

on his system. "You are adorable when you're delirious." I dared to blush. "And I won't hold that against you when you're sane again."

"Do you think Echo would forgive me? If I—If I like her?" He shook, deaf to my words, sweat reflecting the light off his white skin. "Maybe I'm betraying her. Maybe I don't deserve this, after letting Echo—And Shandra broke my nose. There's no way she would care about me. Right?"

"Leon. I am bad at friendship. There's no way I'm ready for dating." That was more Nessa's area. I put my hand to his neck checking his pulse. "And you're otherwise engaged."

"It's been years since Echo— Is it okay to try again?" His words were slurred as he blinked, unable to focus on my figure. "I really want to be happy. Maybe I could start small. Coffee or something?"

"Right. Coffee." I pulled out a bruise salve to increase healing rate, but even as I rubbed it into the cloth, his eyes fluttered closed. In seconds, he was asleep. "Coffee actually sounds nice."

Reality Check

I came to the door to Nessa's apartment. I worked on the lock, swiping my ID card clumsily, letting myself in while balancing two drinks in my hands. It was probably an absurdly dangerous choice, but I'd been more stupid for lesser things.

Granted, getting coffee for a not-boyfriend was probably dumb. There was no way this was how dating worked. Even so, the drinks were in my hands, and I was too busy smiling to listen to my own common sense.

Leon was awake. Finally. Was I supposed to go to him? He stood, his back to me, his hand up against the glass of the dirty window. He lifted his head at the sound of my footsteps, but didn't turn around.

"How do you feel?" That felt like a good question to ask. Very sensitive and all that.

"Like I can breathe again. The bruise is already healing." He put his forehead against the window. "We would have killed for medicine like this at the palace."

"The others are free, now. And you are, too." Should I apologize for his nose? Or was it too long ago? My stomach pinched.

He nodded, turning. After a moment, he noticed my hands.

After an awkward second, I held one of the drinks out to him. He stared, unblinking for a long moment. Finally, he reached a hand out, taking it.

"What did I say last night, when you were treating me?"

I sipped, shocked by the hot, bitter taste. How did Nessa drink this every day? "Not much. You mostly slept—The VitaK will do that to you. Why? Do you remember anything?"

He stared at the lid to his drink. "I remember the shopping plaza, and running without being able to breathe." He swallowed. "How did coffee come up?"

I smiled mysteriously. "Do you not like it?"

"I do, yeah. Of course. I love it. At the palace, I was too low class, and it was a luxury for my superiors. I mean, who gives an animal that? But before, I'd have it every morning. It's always been my thing. I was just worried—do you like this?"

I swallowed another gulp, taking in the hot, sharp tint. "I actually don't normally do coffee. It tastes bitter, and I'm an all or nothing type. It needs to be full of chemicals and practically poisonous, or pure water. Nothing in between. Least of all something that tastes like this."

"But you're still drinking it?"

"I like the smell. It reminds me of Dad." I clamped my jaw shut. I hadn't spoken of my family to anyone, not for years. I didn't even talk to Nessa about them. Those words were not supposed to come out of my mouth.

He took in my expression for a long moment. "Do you want to talk about him?"

My body hurt and I suddenly felt too heavy to continue. I tried to open my mouth, but nothing came out.

"If they were anything like you are, the world was better for having them." He reached a hand out, intertwining his fingers with mine. "Please tell me. I would like to hear about them."

"He was my hero. They both were." I my breath hissed out in a rush. I had been holding this inside for too long. "They actually built MiraCorp as a clinic for the impoverished. They had the best care, the best staff, the most cutting-edge scientists. Almost went broke. They only went into military medicine after the war started, when the World Authority Association told them to. And that's what made millions."

"Nothing like a war to make money." Leon drank.

"Exactly. After the war ended, we had everything we ever wanted. And then a zealot planted a bomb in their lab." It took days to recover their remains. "They'd been working on a new therapy to reach the soldiers with trauma." A weight slipped from my shoulders. "The emergency team told me it was a quick death."

"I'm sorry."

"Yeah." I stared, unseeing. "There was this time, after that, when the company wanted to change their name. But my mom picked MiraCorp. The managers said they didn't care, and it stung." I'd sobbed for days. "I told Nessa about what happened, about how much it hurt. I hadn't even finished, and she was on the warpath. She was going to destroy them for me, remind them who was the boss, and who wasn't. I'd never seen her that mad. But she didn't get the chance. Just in time, my managers recounted, and just changed the logo to a crest of a tree."

Leon's brow darkened. "The crest of the tree is a recent change?"

"As of a few years ago, yes. I'll always remember the image of Nessa, burning with rage as she gave me her opinion. Her hands were formed into fists, and she was pacing in circles, yelling about their idiocy."

Leon nodded, lost to his own thoughts. "She seemed like a good person."

"Seems."

"You really think she's still alive?"

Did I? Really? "Yes."

Mouth of the Beast

The man held the lapels of his white lab coat, a scope viewer attached to the side of his face, a perpetual smile burning into his lips. "That concludes our tour of the main floors. There isn't much more to see, but feel free to observe these two levels on your own." Thus far, we hadn't seen anything suspicious, and I was beginning to doubt this idea of villainy.

He held the door open, certifications and awards hanging beside a large image of the green tree, my brand. "And let me remind you," My guide continued, "That the wonders of MiraSalv 2.0 are groundbreaking. While the original was able to quench bleeding and provide the body with a healing source, it couldn't heal symptoms of starvation. It wasn't a cure all."

"Ah. Interesting." Or incredibly dull.

"But this changes with the next generation of MiraSalv. This form is injected, rather than applied through the skin. It is significantly more aggressive and fights various viruses. When the last of the bugs are ironed out, this drug will change the world." He allowed for a proud smile. "And it will make you, and this company, rich."

"As I would expect." As if I needed more money.

"Of course, you'll want to meet one of our volunteers. I should warn you, Mr. Boston is quite a character, but when we suggested he come, he jumped at the chance. As you can see, we take the role of a volunteer seriously." He pressed a button, speaking into a communicator at his wrist. "Dallas, send in Boston."

A volunteer walked in. Before even an introduction, he flashed a grin that won over even my frozen heart. He wore a suit and tie, the leafy green brand of my company on his nametag. He stepped to a chair, turning it backwards as he sat down.

"Shandra, this is Amon Boston."

"Hello, Gorgeous." He winked at me.

"You're a volunteer," Leon said, incredulous.

"Ooh, yeah." The man flashed a winning expression to my bodyguard, sizing up Leon for a long moment. "Jealous? Unlike you, I don't get paid to stand around, looking smokin' hot. I do that for free. Though I do like your tattoos. Got any more, maybe somewhere scandalous?"

Leon frowned, opening his mouth to snap back. I cut him off. "Why did you volunteer?"

Boston put his hands over his chair, tapping against the metal. "Good question, Beautiful. I had a deteriorating skin condition. It was nasty, too gross for a pretty lady like yourself." He paused obviously. "But then MiraCorp said they were doing trials, and it might save me."

I glanced over his flawless skin. I had a hard time believing this man had ever been anything less than angelic. "It worked, then?"

"Yeah." He leaned closer to me. "I can take my shirt off, show you, if you want. You know, for medical purposes."

"I'm unavailable." Did one coffee with Leon count?

Amon Boston teased his head towards Leon. "Nothing's permanent."

"Boston," the doctor's tone was sharp. "Answer their questions. I'm sure they have other business they need to attend to. You do, too."

The volunteer's nose scrunched, his brow angered. But the look vanished as fast as it came. "What else do you want to know?" Boston's shoulders dropped, sufficiently humbled.

"How are you reimbursed for your time?"

"You mean, other than being alive? They give me a stipend, you know, spending money. And free room and board. It's a nice system. You can stop by my place if you want to investigate further. Maybe tonight."

"Our rewards for their time are according to regulation," the scientist cut in.

I glanced at him, then back to Boston. "How long have you been a volunteer? What do you do here?"

"Oh, it's been at least two years. I come in the morning, and they give a few injections. I hang in the observation rooms. I eat the regulated diet. I'm sure they showed you on the tour, Gemstone."

"Where did you say you lived, again?" The voice came from behind me. Leon. His hand moved unconsciously to his bullet wound.

The man looked up, winking at Leon. "They have quarters for us, set up here, Pretty Boy. You're invited, if you want. But three's a crowd, and I'd rather have the girl."

But this time, Leon's face only hardened. He was silent.

"Alright, alright." He shrugged. "No use in antagonizing you." He held his hand out. "Shake on it? Truce? Let the best man win?"

Leon's lip twitched, flowing back to a blank line almost instantly. But there had been something, whether confusion or surprise, in this sudden expression. His hands remained unmoving.

"Fine then," Boston said, shrugging. "Have it your way. Can't say I tried." He stared at me for only moment, a sudden intensity in his eyes.

I frowned at him, gritting my teeth. But as he closed his fist, I caught a small marking on his right hand, a scribble of ink, light and small, but clear. It was one simple word. *Lies.*

His hand closed, opening again to nothing but blurred ink, his sparkling grin once more across his face as he stared at me. "See you tonight."

"Boston." The doctor's sharp voice rang out with warning. "I think you've said quite enough."

"You're right." He stood suddenly. "Your leave to go?"

The medic nodded his head. In a flash, Boston cut past us, vanishing from view.

The scientist laughed. "I told you he was a lot to take in."

We were allowed to explore the main levels on our own, given our low clearance badges, marked as *owner* and *visitor*. But as we continued our journey, we found nothing out of place. Not where we were allowed, anyway.

Which left us at the exit to the building. Leon grimaced. "Thoughts?" He asked as we stepped to the doors.

"Did you see his hand?"

He nodded once. "It was a dangerous attempt to reach us. If MiraCorp isn't as it seems, and he had to go to those lengths, we have a problem. That was the move of a very desperate man."

"Or very brave."

Leon nodded. "We have to find what's beneath the surface here."

"Agreed. We need to figure out how deep the deception goes. We need to have a look around here, on our own. But how? These badges do nothing for us."

He gave a lopsided smile. "They might. Pass me your badge."

I handed the card over, and he took a small blade, cutting lines in the inscription bar.

"What are you doing?"

"I'm corrupting the ID reader. The electronics will have trouble decoding your digital imprint, and they'll only be able to read that this is an Owner card. The tech will go to default mode, and just let you in. I mean, you do own the place. It would look super bad if the default was set to anything else. Who doesn't let in the owner?"

I shot him a doubtful look.

"I've done this before. At the Palace. I know it'll work."

I stared at him, my eyebrows ruffled.

"People needed medicine." His jaw slammed shut, ending his explanation, and he passed my card back to me. "Now, let's be fast. There's still the cameras to worry about."

Janus

We strode the hallways, passing doctors, their heads buried in paperwork. Busy and unsuspecting, they didn't notice us as out of place as we paced through walkways, peering at security areas.

Finally finding Boston, I peered into a window on the fourth floor, glancing at the proceedings on the other side. He was in a lab, the white walls and counters bleaching his bare skin, the doctor standing next to him. Behind them, on the far side of the room, there was a glowing green symbol of the company, covering the wall, from one side to the other.

"The owner, eh?" Boston asked, turned away from me, his voice thick with an accent. He was hanging the clothing he had been wearing before.

He took a moment to smooth out the costume, then hung it against a sterile cabinet. He grabbed for a threadbare shirt, pulling it on slowly. Fully clothed once more, he crossed his arms, glancing at the stethoscope in the other man's hands.

I could feel a crease of confusion in my brow.

'Yes, indeed, Boston." The doctor tapped his hand against a medical table, gesturing Boston over. "She's taking an interest in her parents' company. Did you like her?"

Grimacing, Boston, moved to the metal shape, staring at the lab table. "More than I like you. But that doesn't take much, now does it."

The doctor began recording vitals, strapping a black wrap around Boston's arm. "Oh, my. I forgot. I'm dealing with a Believer of Serenity. You don't like empty words." He patted the volunteer's face arrogantly.

I bunched my hands into fists, watching, pondering if I should wait until Boston was alone, or if I should barge in now.

Boston, unaware, leaned in, toward the doctor. "Don't pretend you know me."

"Oh, but Amon, I do. Let's see what we have here. Aman Karu, of North Serens." The doctor jabbed in a needle for a blood withdrawal. "You only changed it to Amon Boston once you came here. But you still have that same accent. *Eh?*" He took out the needle, holding it to the light.

Boston's shoulders went rigid. "An accent? Wow. I'm in the presence of a genius."

"Hardly." He wrote into his tablet. "You were one of two children who grew up as a Believer of Serenity. And then you moved here. But NewAmerica does not allow Serenity. All that focus on harmony and departure from technology was secret. When you turned of age, you converted to the Believers of Love, and with it, were forced to abandon your old groupies. After years of struggling down here, you finally got work at a ranch. You were the caretaker of horses that belonged to your master. Or at least, you were, until he sold you to me." He laughed as he put the syringe away. "So much for harmony. Did I miss anything?"

I blinked at the information. Slaves were handed over. Free men were not.

The volunteer, this convert, swallowed, a crack in his façade. "He didn't sell me. It was complicated."

"Betrayal often is." He felt Boston's neck, checking the pulse. "Tell me, do you still cry yourself to sleep, or have you gotten over it?" I was going to give it ten seconds, and then I was barging in, regardless of our plan to pass unnoticed. This doctor needed a lesson in humility.

"At least I can sleep. My conscience is clean. How's yours doing?"

For a long stretch, there was no sound but the scratch of a pen. Finally, he looked up. "Aren't we being disrespectful today. We've talked about this. Should I let the officer contact *her*? Or will a week on half rations do?"

Boston gripped the side of the medical bed, his knuckles whitening. He looked like Leon used to. Cornered.

"Come now. Speak up."

I stood, fury in my motions as I stepped to the door. Leon grabbed my arm, pulling me back, shaking his head. *Not yet*, he mouthed. *Security will find out*. His wide eyes held me from going further. I turned back to the room, breathing out my frustration. This waiting game would be the death of me.

134

"Curse the universe." Boston's voice was suddenly weak, tired. "Half rations."

"Now, let's address the rest of your behavior, shall we?" The doctor put the stethoscope on his ears, reaching under Boston's thin shirt. Boston flinched. "You were told to report any heart abnormalities after your last injection of the salve. But you didn't."

If he was testing MiraSalv 2.0, it had some serious side effects. My lab was apparently destroying people with their trials. Wonderful.

"As such," the doctor continued, "We'll be putting you here, in the observation room, in case the heart problems arise again." He withdrew his tool. "But for now, it sounds like a murmur. Maybe a complication, missing a beat when you're stressed. Maybe you shouldn't be so wound up." He gestured to the adjacent room, past a glass wall.

Boston moved, stepping into his prison. "Monster," he spat.

The doctor locked the observation door behind him. "I wouldn't get all worked up. You know what it does to your heart."

"I know what you did to my heart."

The doctor twisted away, snapping off the light. In a short moment, he stepped into the hallway. Right to where we were.

I was an idiot for being unprepared for this inevitability. As Leon and I backtracked, I probed my brain for what to say. I had to find something to make it look like we belonged here.

But the scientist didn't look up from his notes. He turned in the other direction. Within moments, he was down the hall, lost in his own world. Boston was alone in the dark as the echoing footsteps of the doctor vanished.

"If he's one of their *volunteers*." Leon gestured into the lab, "He might know where Nessa is."

We slipped in. In the shadows, we crept towards Boston, taking in his cage. The symbol of the tree was mounted onto the wall behind him, lit dimly from behind. The illumination tainted the tree red, as if it was on fire. It looked like Stroben's brand.

A sound cut through the air. "Psychopath." The prisoner's voice. His back was silhouetted, a dark shape against the red background, his face hidden.

I froze, Leon behind me. I was not a psychopath. I was rich and powerful, and he was way out line, thinking I was—

He was turned away. He couldn't see us. He didn't even know we existed. He was talking to himself.

"You're going to mess up, and when you do, I'll be there." His voice pitched. "And if not me, someone. Someday soon."

In the darkness, he yelled, a loud banging sound interrupting his tone. He was punching the wall of the cage. He struck again. And again, and again.

His movement cut off abruptly. The silence echoed, and he slipped to the floor. His ragged breathing resounded off the walls. His every breath was an obvious struggle, and he clutched his chest, curling into a fetal position. He looked like someone who was dying.

But... no. Maybe it was the heart problem.

Time slipped through our fingers as we stared at the figure. Slowly, he rose to a sitting position. This was what his condition looked like. Interesting.

"They broke his heart." Leon's voice was loud and raw. "Like they broke mine."

The volunteer froze, going silent.

"Hello, Gorgeous." He turned suddenly as I spoke, drawing to the back of his cage. "That's quite a mark you've got." I gestured to his hand.

He staggered suddenly, gripping wall for support. "You saw it." His voice was weak. "I didn't think—"

"We're on tight schedule," I cut in. I allowed for only a beat of silence, continuing before Leon could say something mildly useless and extremely dramatic. Again. "Security doesn't know we're here yet. Tell me what you know."

He nodded. "Believers are illegally housed in this facility. They're kept in medical observation rooms on the lower levels. They're used as trial cases for the medicine. When an inspector or anyone is brought in, the lead scientist has one of us *volunteer* to speak with him or suffer the consequences. That's how we keep dodging close inspection. We're not allowed to leave, and we can't escape." He turned to me, drawing close for the first time. Here, on the other side of the glass, he wasn't the sexy, sleek, sheen man. He was like ice, broken and cracked, a collection of shattered remnants, glued together through sheer willpower.

"I'm looking for a girl. She's a Believer in Love. Nessa?"

He let time pass. "Are you…" he rethought his words, tapering off into nothingness.

His tone, the sudden reverence, caught me by surprise. "Am I what?"

"I've heard the stories, eh. We all know of the woman in red. She and her companion, they break out people like us. Are you her? Are you the Freedom Dreamer?"

Was I what? This again? No. I was not the Freedom Dreamer. This name was meaningless, but he put stock into the fable, just like Irene.

I glanced to Leon, expecting him to explain that I was little more than a crazy idiot with hate issues. But Leon was silent. He, too, looked at me, waiting for an answer.

"Yeah." Sort of. Not really.

He laughed. "I'm gonna tell everyone how I flirted with the Freedom Dreamer, eh." He took a long breath. "I haven't heard that name before. Eh…do you have any other description to go by?"

"She is a Believer, with the word Agape on her medallion. But she doesn't have it with her right now. She's short. She's got brown hair and brown eyes." Her eyes were brown, right? "She went missing more than eight months ago. She was on flight 472 for a religious thing. Super friendly personality? Boy crazy?"

He laughed. "Agape. Desperate for a boyfriend, but no guy's good enough for her. We do have a woman like that here. Very charming personality. Last I heard, she wasn't doing well." His brow creased. "Are her eyes brown?" He hesitated for only a moment. "Let me out. I'll show you."

Leon nodded, striding over. "Shandra, the mechanics of this lock are like the handcuffs at Stroben's palace. Give me time. I can get him out."

"Stroben's palace? Is my —"

I held a hand up, cutting off Boston. "If we let him out, they'll know he left his cage. The only reason they're not alerted now is because it's dark and we haven't hacked open a prison door." I gestured to the video camera. "And he has a heart problem. He might die on us."

Leon's eyes pleaded, but Boston spoke, gripping the bars with assured confidence. "If you don't let me out, you won't find her."

I glared. That was a bluff. This freak with a heart defect could not use leverage against me. "You're in no condition to argue, Beautiful. The hearsay is that all this stress might kill you." After a heartbeat, Leon stepped back, bowing his head down. I'd upset him. It was annoying that I cared.

Boston's hand crept up to his chest. "I can't let you leave without letting me out. I need to be there, to help save them."

I shrugged, unimpressed. "Thanks for the offer. But we need to be going."

"Shandra." Leon's voice, not Boston's, cut through the air. "We can't leave him. Not like this."

I gave an exasperated huff. "If we open that door, security is going to find out. That is incredibly idiotic, and it would probably get us killed. Is his life really worth that?"

"Was my life?"

Leon's words hung in the air between us, defusing the anger in my arms. The tension in my shoulders faded, and my breathing calmed. He was right. Saving Leon, bringing him with me when I escaped, was reckless and idiotic. But having him with me made it all worth it. "Yes."

After a long pause, Leon stepped up to the control panel to the door. He pried it open and grabbed for two wires. Slowly, allowing me time to stop him, he pressed them together. After a spark, the door slid.

Apparently, this broken-hearted man was going to bring me to Nessa.

Hide and Seek

Boston lead us down two flights of stairs and brought us to a lower level of the building. We stepped into a whitewashed path, striding through a maze of halls and rooms. Finally escaping the maze, we reached a door marked *Unsuccessful Trials*.

"Last I saw her, she was very weak. Are you sure you're ready for this?" Boston's voice rang out as he put his hand on the handle.

I wasn't about to back out now. I nodded.

He opened the door, letting me stride into a room. There was sunlight, from a large window, sprinkling into the room, dust caught in the rays. Past the light, there was a bed stand and a medical wall, surrounding a single area. Beyond the sheet like wall, more sunbeams bounced about creating impression of a bed beyond.

I pulled back the hanging wall. Wrapped in tubes and wires, there was a frail figure. As I drew closer, my footsteps echoed off the stone tiles, mixing with the sound of her life support and the weak beeping of a heart monitor. Her only movement was the slight rising and falling of her chest.

She did not react to my presence. As I took in her pale skin, her tired features, her shallow breathing, she didn't even move.

And then she opened her eyes. They were oceans of green, not blue or brown, accented by whispers of grey. They were crystals and beauty and compassion. They were paintings of life and hope and empathy. They were diamonds in a night sky. But most of all, they were hers, and I had missed them so much.

"Nessa." I traveled continents, fought Brokels, undermined my own company. I drove through deserts, broke slaves out of their pens, uncovered a corrupt company. I had done it all for her. Now, here she was.

She shifted. "No, no, save your strength." I slipped my hand to hers. Faintly, her fingers curled into mine, though her brow illustrated confusion. "Nessa, do you know who I am?"

She swallowed, a movement so pained that I blinked away tears. "Yes." Her voice danced into the silence. "I knew… you'd come." She took a long breath. "Freedom Dreamer."

I blinked. She thought—She thought I was that hero. She thought I was the woman Boston and Irene loved. She thought I was the fables. My eyes began watering, unbidden.

In her eyes, I was someone different. "Nessa," I shoved down a sob. "I'm your friend."

She stared. "Shan?" She smiled, an expression so fragile that it would shatter at the smallest breeze. "I knew you'd come." Her voice was a thread.

I held her hand as a porcelain vase, beautiful, flawless, and fragile. "We're going to save you. You're going to heal and be healthy and happy, and you're going to find that perfect guy you've been

142

talking about, and you're going to get married and live happily ever after…" my voice evaporated.

She took a breath. My world was falling apart. All I wanted was to see her, and it finally happened. But her broken body was slumped, tied to fluids.

I grabbed for the heartbeat monitor on her hand, pulling it off. I turned to the saline solution, gripping the IV, preparing to pull it out of her.

"Shandra, no." Leon's hand covered mine. "She shouldn't be moved."

"She's alive. She'll be fine, just as soon as we get her away from here." My voice squeaked. The knots in my chest were making it hard to breathe.

He pried my fingers from the IV. "She's not strong enough."

"She's always been strong enough." I'd finally found her. Why did it hurt this much? I found Nessa, and I couldn't save her. "Leon?" Panic was bleeding into my voice.

"We'll think of something."

"We can't move her." As I spoke, a red light flashed out. A warning light. Security must have noticed Boston was free.

Leon looked over her. "Nessa can't be moved. At least not right now. We need to go. We can come back again in a few days, when the security has mellowed out, and we can find a way to move her."

"She doesn't have days." She didn't have hours left.

"Shan…" a voice whispered. "Shan?"

"Nessa, please. Save your strength. We're going to find a way. We're going to…" I had no idea what we were going to do.

She shook her head, the slightest tilt of her chin the only movement. "No. You're… you're the Freedom Dreamer. Do…. What you came for. Destroy this burning tree."

"I came for you. I searched the world for you."

The light flashed above her, bathing her in painful red. "Save us," she whispered. "Save us all."

Time froze. Nessa was going to die. Nothing short of a miracle would save her. But what she was asking was too much. I could not save the others. "I don't know how."

She didn't react, and her eyes peacefully closed. My breath caught, worried that she might be…. But no, there was still a shallow lifting of her chest.

Boston coughed in the doorway. "We could do it. They have footage of their experiments. If tech boy here has the skills, eh," he gestured to Leon, "then he could splice the videos together and put it in a file, we could send it out." He crossed his arms. "The authorities could be here within the hour if they saw it. I mean, Believers are just third-class citizens, but we aren't animals."

"A broadcast?"

"Something to use as evidence against this whole company."

Leon cut in. "I can do it. I once rewired a transport's motherboard. This won't be much harder. How would we find the footage?"

"A security control room. We could break in, splice some videos together, and send it out. The news would eat that like candy. I just don't know if we have enough time." He gestured to the lights overhead.

I glanced back at Nessa. If this was her last request, I would grant it or die trying. "I'll be back for you." My hand brushed by my pocket. Her Medallion. I took it out. "Hang in there." I pressed it back into her hands, swallowing the pain in my chest. This wasn't goodbye.

I turned to Leon. "You aren't a part of this. You should leave now. Finding Nessa was one thing, and you accomplished that. But taking down this company? You've already been shot and, and you're still healing. This is asking too much of you."

"The bruising hasn't slowed me down so far." The reformed Favored One folded his arms. "If you're going, I'm going."

"No," I hissed. "Now isn't the time to get all prideful on me. I—"

"This isn't pride." He gave a small smile. "This is friendship. This is what friends do for one another."

"No. Friendship is getting coffee and laughing together. This is not that."

He jutted his chin out. "Friendship is being there for someone. Philos."

"Eh, wow," a voice said from across the room. Boston. "A philosophy debate. Now's a perfect time. Except not. Security. Flashing lights." He turned on his heel, leaving the room.

I followed him, my steps pounding against the laminated floor. Much to my chagrin, Leon followed suit.

Part IV Death, Us Part

Shut Down

"I want to see our visual files on Test Subject 811," I spat, stepping into the lab. Light from the three windowed walls struck me, filtered by shadows of tech stands and screens. "Let's see it." There were tablets, hand screens, ports mounted to stands. Leon would be able to work with this.

I glanced to a single door, marked *rooftop*. If things went south, that could be an escape route. But with only two employees in the room, they wouldn't be too much to handle.

"Excuse me?" A guard's voice cut in from the corner. He could be an issue.

"Are you deaf? I own this company. When I say I want visual files, you get me visual files." My voice was thick and stern, overboard. Even I wasn't convinced.

"I don't have time for this," he said, gesturing to the door. "I don't care who you are. If it's not cleared by Dallas, I don't deal with you."

I was about to retort, but my voice caught. That name meant something to me. Whatever it was, it left a sour taste in my mouth. His name stung my chest. But where had I heard it before?

My eyes flashed up. Dallas was the name of the officer who told me Nessa was dead. This security man got his orders from Dallas. What if it wasn't just any Dallas, but *the* Dallas? What if it was the officer from Stroben's castle, working here? What if he was intentionally keeping me from finding Nessa? MiraCorp had invested serious resources in lying to me.

I gritted my teeth, sucking in a swallow of air. It tasted like betrayal.

The officer gestured again to the exit, but with a flare of anger, I stepped up to him. I grabbed the taser strapped to my leg, stabbing his chest hard. Sparks flew. He fell to the floor, stunned.

I moved to the people at the electronics. I stepped up to the man, slamming his chair over to knock him to the ground. I went at him with a sudden flow of blows, but I was distracted by a movement from my peripheral. The other worker yanked on a lever. In response, the room was bathed in a squawking sound. Slowed by his chest wound, Leon drew out his stun rod, slamming it into the woman. Within a second, the useless and annoying girl fell.

I caught the man in my grip, slamming my fist into his face. There was a solid thump, but no cracking sound, nothing that would kill him. Just enough to keep him from waking up soon.

With three unconscious persons on the floor, I waved Boston in, my hand burning from my own punch. "We need this to stay locked," I slammed it closed behind him. "Can you handle a gun?" He was the only one of us who was unarmed.

He nodded with no hesitancy, so I pulled the guard's weapon out of the holster, handing it to him. "I think the door is bulletproof, but if anyone gets through, just point and shoot." After switching off the alarm, I turned to Leon. "How are we doing?"

"Good, I think." Already sitting at the electronics, he pulled a transportable dataholder out of a tech drawer. He plugged it into one of the machines. Instantly, a security screen popped up, and Leon's brow darkened as he began typing. "This won't be fast. How much time do we have?"

In answer, there was a barrage of fists against the locked entrance to the room, followed by a string of shouts and furious utterances.

"Not much," We didn't have an escape plan. "We may need it to be fast."

He dipped his chin distractedly, still typing symbols into the screen. Then the speaking began, muffled by the door. A voice. "Leon, open up. This doesn't have to be this way."

I could feel my face whitening. Koren.

Leon jerked his head. "How—

"Surprised? We were too, when the good doctor called, telling us about a man with slave tattoos scribbled on his face. I just had to come see for myself."

Leon gagged, running his hand over the markings. I hadn't even noticed them since the palace. I'd been an idiot for not making him hide that tattoo.

Boston glanced over. "Guys, I'm not sure staring at the door will help. Eh?"

Leon locked his attention back to the screen, attempting to refocus, but his jaw was quivering. All Koren needed was to say a word, and he'd slither inside Leon's head. Being a torturer had that effect on people.

"Um, okay," I said, speaking loudly into Leon's ear, trying to hide my panic. "It's cool. You're with me, okay, not them. All you need to do is get past the security screen and load the files."

Leon's fingers started shaking. "I need a digital key card from one of the tech guys," he said, gesturing in that direction.

I nodded, squatting over the unconscious man to find the card.

Koren continued. "I know you can hear me, Favored One. Ceba's here, too. Do what we say, and it'll all go smoothly. We could even ignore your new girlfriend's little feud with Stroben, pretend we never saw her. No one needs to be hurt." There was a long pause. "Well, no one but you."

I passed the card to Leon. He swallowed as he slid it into the screen, a new wrinkle of desperation in his features. "Shandra, I can't—I can't do this fast enough. He's going to get in. He's going to—" He scrunched his eyes closed in an overwhelmed horror.

I was trying to come up with a backup plan, but it wasn't looking good. Everything was falling apart, and Leon was unraveling, and Boston was

150

probably going to have a heart attack. Maybe the shutting down, giving in to the threat was not a bad idea.

The security screen glowed green and we were inside, files popping up before us. "We need to find files that look incriminating, and slap them on the drive. Let's just keep working." Maybe we'd get extremely lucky, like at the palace. Doubting my own thoughts, I gripped my weapons.

"Ceba brought some Deprov. She was excited when the company called us to report that our missing slave was snooping around in their buildings, tattoo marking and all. Stroben's been clear about just how much we can mess you up. Ceba's thrilled, but you know it doesn't need to be like that." Koren laughed echoed through the door. "Leon, open the door. Do it now, or we're going to take this places we don't want to go."

Leon stopped, pulling his hands away. After a long breath, he shook his head. "They are not going to win. Shandra, I need you to prepare that second screen," he gestured to the vacant one beside him, "We don't have enough files yet, and we're running out of time."

This wasn't my area of expertise, but I sat down.

There was the sound of footsteps on the other side of the door. Someone had joined Koren and Ceba. "Boston's in there, isn't he?" The scientist.

I breathed in relief. All Amon Boston had to do was shoot people if they got through. He could probably handle the distraction, unlike Leon.

No one could get under his skin. Right? I sped up my process.

"Amon, if you don't open the door, we're going to have to *take measures.*"

Boston shoulders dropped. "Eh." There was a long space of silence. "You won't find her." I glanced up, hoping that his unsure reaction was a stalling tactic. But the resignation, brought on by a single line, was not comforting.

I stood, grabbing for my taser. He had a distance weapon, while mine was short range. I had to be subtle. I had to walk over calmly, carefully, counting on the distraction of the voices.

"Come now," the scientist hissed. "I told our friends we won't need back up. You'll do as you are told. Remember what's important to you. All those cute notes she sends make her easy to track. Think about your options."

Boston's face paled. "She'll hide. Or get away. She'll keep herself safe." He pressed his hand to his chest, as if he could feel a heart... thing coming on.

I continued closer, still unnoticed. There was the sound of sparks and a small explosion on the other side. The entrance didn't open, but smoke leaked in between the bottom of the door and the floor.

"Your sister, safe? Let's see. Stroben's Palace, out in the NewSahara. A food server, if I'm not mistaken. In fact, I bet I could have her flown in within a day." As Koren gave a muffled curse, the scientist continued in his litany of destruction. "We'd have to bring her here. We'd have her join

152

the testing program." A fist slammed into the door. "If you don't open this, I'll make you watch it all."

He had someone at the palace? And they knew where this person was? He was going to betray us. Almost close enough to strike him now, I gripped my weapon.

Boston lifted his gun, pointing it to my chest. "Drop it," he hissed, his voice tight, not bothering to look my way. "Just drop it."

I heard my taser clatter to the ground as I spoke. "You can't let them in."

He shook his head, his eyes watering. "You don't understand. They don't make empty threats here. I can fight back every day, pretend I can take it, pretend it doesn't destroy me. I can play their games and twist their words. I can ruffle their feathers and antagonize them. But they're always going to have her. So they're always going to win."

The scientist continued. "Amon, all you need to do is press a button, and the girl can stay safe. Do you really want everything you endured to be for nothing?"

"You won't find her." His voice wavered. "She'll know you're coming."

"Are you willing to bet your sister's life on that?"

Leon hit the screen a few more times. "I got it, I got it," he yelled, his voice tripping on itself. "The data's on the drive. We can send it out now. It'll just take—

The door hissed open.

Out of Darkness

Boston had his hand on the entrance button to the door. He glanced up without expression. "She's all that's left of my family."

If I wasn't preoccupied with the slavecatchers, I would end his life.

Instead, I stood my ground, unarmed. Behind us, Leon jumped to my side, leaving the datacarrier still plugged in to the screen. Fumbling, he grabbed for his weapon, but his terror was obvious. Amon Boston had already dropped his gun, kicking it over, not to the scientist, but to the man who came in behind him.

Officer Dallas. Officer Seth Dallas. The instrument of my own company's manipulation. A wave of fury shook me. As I stepped in front of Leon, Dallas stepped over to Boston, putting a hand on his shoulder. "You did the right thing. I knew you would. I didn't want us to have to bring her into this. You know I hate that idea."

Boston's fingers gathered into fists. "I have no idea how you live with yourself."

"Luna Storm," Koren hissed, stepping up to me as I cursed my empty fists. *Where was my taser?* "We cross paths once more. I think our last meeting didn't live up to my expectations. This time, things will go as planned."

"You've been a very naughty girl." Ceba drew out a laser gun, aiming it at me. "Stroben wants you alive. Pity, that you got caught in the crossfire.

Koren and I tried so hard not to kill you, now, didn't we." She laughed. "Any last words?"

She was serious. They were going to shoot me. Leon pulled me back, sliding in front. "Ceba, no. Please." His words were sapped and without dignity. "Please. Don't—

I heard, more than felt, the blast coming at me. There wasn't much light or sound.

I wouldn't have noticed that it even happened, except for the strike of agony.

And then—And then—And then I felt nothing. I knew nothing. I was nothing. I was—

I was standing in my apartment, from long ago, Nessa twirling in a borrowed dress. "How do I look? If I'm not pretty enough to make them all fall in love with me, I need to know."

Wearing a formal blue dress myself, I blinked at her. "As your best friend, I feel it's my duty to say you look great." My voice was bland, bordering on sarcasm.

She snorted. "Thank you. Now, as a critic?"

"You look fine." I stared in the mirror at my reflection. I hadn't worn a dress like this, such dark colors, since the funeral. It'd been years, but even so, it didn't feel complete without tears.

How was it possible that it still hurt this much?

She stepped over, smoothing over her fiery red skirt as she looked into the mirror, too. "You look beautiful, too. Elegant. They would be proud of the woman you've become."

I blinked away the water in my eyes. "I don't care what I look like." I swallowed hard. "And I don't care about what anyone thinks of me, living or dead. They wouldn't be proud of me. You wouldn't be, either."

She took my hand as her brow lowered. "You are made for greatness. I know you can't see it yet, but I can."

"You're wrong."

She smiled. "Am I?" As she moved, she knocked into a vase, a priceless Serens Original, sending it to the floor.

Instead of screaming, I snorted. It was an ugly vase.

What she said meant more to me than that useless art did. But her words were wrong. I wasn't a hero. I was lying on the floor of the lab. I'd been shot, and I was dying. Greatness would have kept going, chosen to live, to fight, to endure, despite it all. But I couldn't choose that path. I wasn't strong enough.

Was I?

Sound. A muffled grunt. Pain leaking through growing seams. And something else. Something important. Something outside of myself, something I cared for. Someone.

Leon. My eyes snapped open, letting in the pain of light and dark and memories.

I had been stunned, not killed. My skin crawled with a numbness, but there was no blood. I would make it. Apparently, Ceba wanted me alive.

156

I took in a confused garble of color. There were figures, one kneeling on the floor, two standing over it. The female held a gun, pointing it at the kneeling man's head. The other knelt down next to the slave, running his hand through his hair. *It's a tranquilizer,* he hissed, a voice distant and disjointed with the mouth of the specter. *Picture it. You, helpless, at our feet.*

The figure, Leon, struggled against the bindings around his arms and legs, screaming at his captors. Then there was the sound of the weapon firing, powerful, distant, and strange.

We'll take him to the transport, the man said, coming into focus. "Then let's come back for the girl."

Koren picked up an unconscious Leon, throwing the slave over his shoulder. His movements efficient, he stepped out, the woman following him.

I lifted my head, vision fluttering. I could barely breathe, much less fight. I was drooling on the floor, my fingers rejecting my demands for movement. I would scream in rage, but my mouth refused to move. I loathed my own helplessness.

But in the spectrum of hate, my own weakness did not trump Boston. His own cowardliness was what brought us here. The fact Koren and Ceba had Leon again burned my thoughts. The very thought of Stroben engulfed my mind in rage.

Even so, I had nothing left to fight with. Koren and Ceba were coming for me. Standing at a lab table, Dallas and the scientist were gesturing to the technology, speculating at our aim.

But there was another person, wasn't there? My brain cleaned itself of the fog, and I saw the form of Boston. He was picking up my taser, removing it from my reach. His movements were robotic, destroyed.

I drooled on the floor, I couldn't help but loathe him. "I'm sorry. I can't be like you. I can't save everyone. I can't be the Freedom Dreamer."

Officer Dallas stepped over. "That's right, Amon. You can't. In fact, you can't even save your sister. Those two experts," he gestured to where Koren and Ceba were, "Work for your sister's boss." I wasn't sure I heard him right. "It's how we were able to call them in so fast. I'd recognize the tattoos of the slaves of Stroben anywhere."

Boston's shoulders froze, confusion in his brow. "What?"

Dallas patted him on the back. "They're from Stroben's Palace. In fact, the one they took away, Leon, is a personal favorite. I bet he knows your sister."

Boston's jaw worked as he stepped back. After a swallow, he spoke to me. "You're a slave?"

"No," I couldn't get my voice past a whisper. "Leon is. I'm not." Would he be forced to attend my execution? Would Stroben make Leon try to kill me? Or would they settle for enslaving me?

"My sister. Do you, eh… did you see her?" He gripped the taser with white knuckles, suddenly vulnerable.

I let his words wash over me. Who would—

"Irene." Ironic that she saved me so he could hand me to my executioners. My laugh caught in my throat. It wasn't as funny when I was the one going to die.

Boston's face flushed with horror. I almost felt bad for him. Almost. "You have the same accent. *Eh*." I propped myself to a sitting position.

He tilted his head, paling with fear. "Is she, eh, okay? Alive?"

"As okay as Leon was. That is, before you and Koren captured him." I wrapped my arms around me, realizing my ability to move was improving dramatically. "Last I knew, she was in NewIstanbul, free. She escaped from Stroben."

He fiddled with my taser in his hands for a long moment, indecision in his eyes. "Free?"

I nodded sharply. "I saved her, Boston, and you threw Leon back into that hell."

His chest caved. He glanced back to the scientist and Officer Dallas, lowering his voice. "And if you had the chance to find her again, could you?"

I snarled. "I suppose we'll never know." And it served him right.

"Maybe." He stepped over to the two men, who were working at the electronics, but he was still focused on me. "If you are lying about my sister, you will regret it."

As he drew closer, the scientist remained unaware, his hand pressed against the metal. Dallas noticed, leaning on the desk as he turned.

"Amon, hand me that weap—

With a swiping motion, Boston reached his hand out, pulling the dataholder away, stabbing the desk. The current from the taser traveled along, reaching its tendrils into the hands of the two men, pouring into their fragile hearts, electrifying their systems. The energy sparked and burned flesh and metal before Boston pulled the weapon away. Dallas and the scientist slipped to the floor, thoroughly neutralized.

Boston glanced to my flabbergasted features as I spoke. "Did you just… kill them?"

"I know how much the human heart can take." He put his hand on his chest. "Trust me, it won't be fun, but they'll live."

I wasn't sure. But I was no expert.

"If I help you send this," He was holding up the dataholder. "to the media sites, you will help me find my sister?"

"How about you help me, and I don't fry what's left of your heart." I shakily got to my feet. "And besides, you burnt up our electronics. We can't send it out now."

"There's an antenna, probably on the roof. I think. It's how they send and receive so much data. They're a lab, they have to have one. We could connect on the roof."

160

"How would we connect a dataport to an antenna?"

"All we'd need is a way to connect the current or something, right? A wire would work." He bent over the fried screens, staring at the guts of the machines. "This would be easier with a technician."

"I have practically no tech skills. Leon would have been helpful. Too bad someone backstabbed him."

He met my eyes with less guilt than he should have. "Then we'll do it without him. We've got to try."

Undone

We stepped onto the roof, my chest heaving from the residual effects of the stun.

"We had better be able to do this, Boston. Where's this rod we're going to use?" Had it been slightly closer to the ground, or perhaps slightly safer up here, this environment would have been beautiful. But it was a treacherous rooftop.

Boston took in the surroundings, and then pointed to a beam towards the edge. "It's there," his voice was almost drowned out by the wind. "I think. We can pry the panel on the side, eh. We should find a dataport we can plug it into. Past that, we just need enough electricity to send the files. How hard could that be?"

He didn't sound confident, but pointing it out would do us no favors. "Make it fast. Koren and Ceba have to be on their way back by now."

He took the hint, striding forward with purpose. Within moments, he was prying away metal, spilling open wires and ports.

"You know what this all does?"

I doubted he heard me over the gusts, but he nodded, a slight movement. "Eh, sort of." His tone was distracted. "You talking doesn't help."

Annoyed, I pressed my lips together. This was—

The door to the roof tore open. The sound of it, with the cry that followed, was so loud that it breached the overwhelming torrent.

I dove behind one of the smoking towers. In a quick movement, I looked out, taking in the attackers. But as I saw them, I froze. They didn't have weapons drawn.

I stopped, standing in the open area. The gusts died, and silence settled over the battlefield.

Koren was tranquil, at ease with task of kidnapping humans. He gripped Leon's hair, forcing the slave below him. Ceba was ready for a fight, craving in her eyes. In an excited gesture, she reached for two of her knives, flashing a Cheshire grin.

And Leon. His head was tilted upwards, relieving the tug on his hair. Before, he had been wearing the tan armor, but now I could see the raw bruises. The clothing did not cover the red lashes across his chest. It did not cover the purple splotches that decorated his face and neck. It did not cover the way his jaw quivered before he spoke. "Koren, you hate me, not them. Let them be. They have nothing to—"

"Shut up." The monster kicked the Favored One

Leon lost his voice, shrinking in on himself. I took a rageful step forward. "You're going to regret that."

"I'm sure." Koren brought his attention to me. "Imagine my surprise when security told me that you escaped. I mean, Dallas is an idiot for underestimating you. But when they said you were on the roof, with the dataholder, I had to deal with you myself. You do have a price on your head, you know."

"If you want me, come and get me." I drew out my taser.

"That trick of yours won't work again." He laughed. "No. I don't need to come to you."

He knelt, pushing Leon against one of the rods. He pulled out a pair of handcuffs, slapping them onto the Favored One's wrists, chaining him.

I should have been terrified for him. But I looked at Leon's chafed, bleeding wrists, the swollen bruise on his face, the marks across his skin. A burst of anger flowed through me. I was going to end Koren.

"You see, Leon," He grabbed the man's jaw, forcing Leon to look at the him. "I'm going to break you apart until your girlfriend gives in. How long do you think that ought to take? Four seconds? Five?"

Leon held the slavecatcher's gaze. "Koren, this has nothing to do with her. This is about me. Your job is to get me, not her. I'm the Favored One. She just—"

Leon went silent as Koren slammed his fist forward. The slave smashed his head back into the pole. It did nothing to save him from the incoming blow. A clang echoed across the roof as I flinched.

"I told you to stop," I screamed at him.

Ignoring me, Koren stared into his hazel eyes. "She struck a Brokel. I am bringing her back, and she is going to die. Horribly. At Stroben's own hand. Or maybe yours."

Leon bowed his head as his nose began to bleed. "Koren, no. Listen to me. You're the slavecatcher, and I'm the slave. Your job is me, not her." His tone was nasally, blood decorating his face. "Don't get sidetracked."

"Oh, and now you're looking out for me?" He reached his hand out, petting Leon. "Why don't you shut your pretty mouth before I break it?"

Leon trembled as Koren held him. "Leave her be. Please."

Unadulterated rage poured through me. I would not let him go back to what he was. And he wasn't going to beg to Koren. Not now. Not ever. "Get your hands off him."

Koren allowed for a leer of victory before he turned. "Or what?"

"Or I'll make you." This was what he wanted. He wanted me to engage, to give him a chance to taste blood. He wanted to have fun bringing me to Stroben. I just didn't care.

As Ceba moved past to confront Boston, Koren, seeing me pause, snorted. With a strike of his fingernails, he drew a line of red down Leon's face. Leon choked back a scream.

Ignoring the girl, I flew at Koren, swinging in a fury. He dodged easily, expecting such an obvious bout. But I was better at this than he knew. My real attack was a kick aimed to his knee.

Staggering for a moment, he backed up a step, anger in his expression. With a sudden jab forward, he swung a succession of punches toward me.

Each throw was powerful and difficult to block, and already, I could feel my arms bruising. But I wasn't about to give up.

He pressed forward. I retreated with each of his aggressive moves.

I glanced to Boston, now in combat with Ceba. His peaceful upbringing, his Serenity background, was obvious as he took a blow to the face. At the last second, Ceba pulled back, tripping him instead. The slavecatcher was playing with him. Even if I won this fight, Boston would lose.

I turned back. Koren knew his territory well, and he was pushing me to the edge. I would have to disengage and redirect the attack. I was going to have—

"He begs on cue, you know." Koren's tone was mocking. He struck out again. "And you'd be shocked at the things he's done, just for five minutes free from me. Sold out friends. Ratted on slaves. Gotten them killed. Has he told you about it all?"

Rage boiled through my veins. "Lies." I blocked him.

He gave an exasperated laugh. "You really know nothing about him, do you? Granted, how could you? You can't know a person until they've seen the tools, the knives and scalpels. You don't know them until they've drooled blood onto your hands.

166

You can't know the Favored One until he's given up everything that matters, just for five minutes away from the pain."

I was going to kill him. I stepped forward and lunged at him, but he mirrored the move, and I was forced to draw back once more. I was hazardously close to the edge. I had to get myself out of here—

"He sold out his girlfriend. Did he tell you that?" He swung at me, pulling out his laser.

I kicked at it, and it flew out of his hands, to where Ceba and Boston were fighting. "She was hidden when he tried to poison Stroben." He grinned. "It was a good spot, too. She might have lived, if your boyfriend didn't blab."

I couldn't disengage. I had to slaughter him. I threw three more fast bouts at him, but he still continued forward. I took another pace back, feeling my foot hang in the open air.

I had let this continue for too long. I was in trouble. I shifted back, too close.

He threw a fist into my face, one I dodged easily. As I blocked, I felt a foot around my knee, pulling me to the ground, right on the edge.

My body half over the open air, I scrambled away, but his attack continued. He sent a knee into my face, and I saw, felt, knew nothing but blinding stars. I was slipping from reality.

Only pure willpower brought me back. As I shook myself out of the trance, he put a hand around my throat. "After that first jab, I thought you might be a challenge. But it was easy to distract you. Is Leon such a weakness of yours?" He snarled. "Though I see why you like him. He's so eager to please."

I couldn't breathe. He was going to kill me, or worse, bring me back. It almost didn't matter. Nothing did, not as much as the pain.

I clawed at his fingers, but in response, he only pressed harder around my skin. The world shifted into a foggy, blurred smog. A burning desperation laced its way through me as I tried to breathe.

"Oh, my." He shook my neck, a movement that brought my attention back. "It's the Favored One. He's watching. Over there. Begging me to stop." He gestured with his eyes. "Right on cue. Can you hear him? Beg, dog."

I followed the gaze, taking in the scene as my lungs screamed. There was Leon, cuffed to the rod, pleading with Koren. He was crying, tears streaming down his face as he stuttered, desperation in his expression.

The edges of my vision began creeping in. I struggled one final time, but with no success. I couldn't shake him.

Leon was screaming now, begging Koren, but his pledges meant nothing. Koren knew he could take whatever he wanted from Leon. The slave had no leverage. He was, as he was meant to be, powerless. A dog.

I felt my limbs slacken. "Oh, that last offer of his sounds fun." Koren stared deep into my fading soul. "Imagine me, owning the rights to this

Favored One, having him under my thumb forever. Maybe I'll have him bury your body, as my first instruction as his new master."

The darkness closed in, finally dulling the agony.

Paris Once More

Air rushed in. I curled on my side, surprised, gasping, sucking oxygen past my swollen throat. Being alive was a luxury I hadn't expected, even with the burning webs that spun down my chest, torching my lungs. After a few breaths I stumbled to my knees, trying to prepare for another attack. I had to be ready when he tried to finish the job.

As I lifted my head, I saw him grappling with Leon. My mind struggled through the pain. How was Leon free?

Stumbling to my feet, I sprawled into Koren, knocking him to the ground as I shoved Leon away. My hands fumbling, I managed to wrap my arms around the monster's neck, keeping him down. He was seething pure fury, but that would soon fade into desperation.

"How does it feel, knowing you're about to die?" My words were little more than a croak.

He attempted to dislodge my grip, but once more, he underestimated my resolve.

"Hear that?" I rasped painfully over the wind. "Leon's not offering anything anymore."

Paces away, Leon was pulled back by a furious Ceba. I glanced to Boston, who was supposed to be fighting her, but he was slumped on the ground. He was clutching his chest, his face twisted in rage at his own weakness.

I had Koren quelled, and Boston wasn't about to move. The only wildcard was Leon. I glanced over to him. Ceba threw three quick punches at him. He attempted to block, but his movements were slow, confused, unpracticed. She pulled out a pair of silver knives, stabbing one into his calf. He screamed, but she reached up, pressing the other into his neck. "How did you get out?" She drew a thin line of red over his neck. A warning. But I was in no position to help him.

Leon laughed, shaking from his wounds. "You handcuffed me." He attempted to pull away, but she held fast. "I'm Stroben's Favored One. I have worn cuffs and collars, and chains for years. I learned how to take them off. All I needed was time, and you gave me ample amounts."

Ceba, unaware of Koren's struggle, struck Leon hard with her free hand, leaving a flush of red across his face. "Favored One, you've forgotten your place. Let me remind you."

"Him and Koren both." My voice was raw but full of rage.

She glanced at me, pausing. Her eyes widened as her expression faltered. But she recovered quickly, snarling at me. "If you kill him, I'll slaughter the experiment." She was firm and angry, frozen, her focus on my unwavering fingertips around Koren's neck. Dropping the knife, she pulled out two guns, aiming them at Boston. "I mean, the Favored One we want alive, but this man is expendable."

For his part, Boston, evidently alive, had somewhat recovered, clutching his chest as he sat up, near Koren's fallen laser. "Do it. I don't care," he hissed, his voice thin with pain. "Freedom Dreamer, I'm not worth it. Don't stop."

Ceba knew the determination in his tone. "Fine, then. I'll kill the boyfriend." Training one pistol at Boston, she pressed the other to Leon's forehead. "And then we can be alone, you and I both."

"Koren needs to die," I hissed. I hated that he hunted me, that he had been after Leon for so long, that he was a slavecatcher. I hated that he took pleasure in the pain of others. I hated him. He couldn't be allowed to exist in this world.

I expected her to continue threatening to the end, but she didn't. Instead, Leon found his voice, pushing her away. "She really will kill him. Ceba, just let me talk to her."

He pulled away. Ceba kept her weapon pointed at him, her hands shaking, but she didn't shoot. He drew close to me. "Shandra, He looks subdued. I'm sure the government officials can deal with it. The World Authority Association can handle it." His voice was tight with pain. "You don't need to kill him. Please stop."

I glanced at the monster, watching his pale face as his eyes fluttered closed. "He's a demon. Or do you not feel the bruises?" I gestured to Leon's beaten torso.

He flushed deeply. "I feel everything." He gulped in a long breath. "All of this hurts. Shandra, please. Get off him. Please. You're not…. Not this. You aren't Koren. You're not Ceba. You're not

Stroben. Please. You're not another warlord. Please be better than that."

"Leon, he—

"I don't care what he did," Leon's eyes filled with tears as he moved closer. "He's insane, and he's sick, like Stroben, and there's genuinely something wrong with all of them. I care about you, and I care that you're not like them."

"Leon," I whispered, my voice weak.

"Shan," he said, reaching his hand out. "I think you're better than this. I know you are."

"No. I'm not. I own MiraCorp, a system that enslaves humans. Leon, I am exactly like her."

He wrapped his arms around mine, willing my grip to release. "I don't care about your past, Shandra. I don't care who you were. I care who you are right now. Right now, you are not Stroben."

"Not Stroben? Leon, I don't know who I am, if I'm not that. What even am I?"

He peeled my arms away from Koren.

"You get to be free, just like me."

The Truth

A laser bolt stuck Ceba, and she fell, writhing before she went still. A stun bolt. Boston, crouching on the ground, tossed Koren's weapon to the side, exhaustion and pain in his features. "Again, with the philosophy. Next time, do your soul-searching when my life's not on the line."

After a long space of silence, he stood, moving to her, checking her pulse. Apparently healed, he grabbed her communicator. His movements slow, he made a call to the authorities. He glanced to me once, while the tones rang out. "I hope we're square, now."

I snorted. "You've got a long way to go before I trust you." The wind picked up, then settled again. "But shooting Ceba was a step in the right direction."

The emergency personnel answered, and Boston turned away.

Leon stepped over. He wrapped his arms around my shaking shoulders, bringing me to him. "I knew you'd make the right choice."

I gurgled out a weak laugh, my body trembling. "That makes one of us." I nestled my head into his shoulder.

He held me, turning his lips to my ear. "You aren't a killer. You aren't evil. You aren't Stroben."

I dared to hope that maybe one day, I could even be good.

The NewAmerican team came within minutes, flying onto the rooftop. Rushing, the lead medic stepped forward, nodding to me. "Shandra Lux?"

"Yes." A group of security medics gathered Koren and Ceba, moving them to stretchers. "What will happen to them?"

The medic ran a hand through her hair, glancing over. "They'll be treated, then transported to a World Authority legal complex." She reached out, feeling my neck. I winced. "You should be worried about yourself."

I coughed, pushing her away. "You have other test subjects in the building." Like Nessa. "They need immediate attention."

She pursed her lips, pulling a communicator to her side, turning to the side as she spoke. After issuing a few orders, she turned back to me. "How'd your neck—"

"That man," I pointed to Boston. "just had a heart attack." She stepped away, leaving me in peace.

I turned away, grateful for the knowledge that heart conditions were usually treated first. Rubbing my bruised chin, I stepped over to Leon, watching a young medic inject him as he sat on a medical stretcher. "The sedative should kick in soon."

His hand went to his face. "I think my nose needs to be set, too." Inspecting for damage, she pressed against a bruise on his chest. He winced.

"One thing at a time." She brushed her red hair out of her face. "And that can be done when you won't feel it." She moved to the bruising around his wrists.

He nodded, swaying. "Wow. These NewAmerican drugs."

"Lean back." She grabbed his shoulder, easing him down. "Now, let's see to these wounds." She grabbed a disinfectant out of her med bag, rubbing it into his cuts.

I stepped next to him, wrapping my fingers around his. "How are you feeling?"

He smiled, a confused, weak smile. "I feel like we won." His words were slurred. "Nessa would be proud." He sighed, closing his eyes. "What's next for us?"

"After you heal? First off, I think you'll need a few more shirts," I allowed for a smile. "But after that? I'm not sure. I hear there's an old mechanic's shop down the road from my place. They're looking for a new owner."

He smiled. "Want me to stay?"

"Having a friend around would be nice. Besides, if you leave, who's going to fix my transports when I'm running from slavecatchers?"

He laughed, then flinched. "You can't even fix your own splash shield." He snorted. "I'll teach you one day. Now, what was that about new shirts?"

176

Epilogue

Nessa hadn't woken up. It had been over a week since we'd moved her out of MiraCorp, and the doctors said she had a chance of survival. But it wasn't certain.

I was sitting with her in the hospital room. It was eerily like the MiraCorp labs, but I'd brought in fresh blankets, pots of flowers, strange Believer quotes. Anything to make it less clinical.

She hadn't woken, but things were looking better. There was a possibility she might wake. She was even stable now. She even—

"She was something." Boston stood at the doorway. "And when she was the one you were looking for, I wasn't even surprised. Of course, a woman like that would be a friend of the Freedom Dreamer. Although her eyes are not brown."

I lifted a brow. "Are you correcting the Freedom Dreamer?"

He laughed, taking a seat on the other side of Nessa. "Only when you're wrong."

"You literally stopped by to tell me that I was wrong about her eyes?" I snorted. "You're the worst."

"Actually, I didn't come for you." He drew a single rose out, placing it on Nessa's stand.

My jaw dropped. "You two were..." There was no way I missed that.

"No." He laughed softly. "Love was impossible there." He swallowed, a hard motion. "We were fighting our hardest, every day. Every hour, every minute, every second was a war. We could only have one hope, and that was escape. So we battled, side by side, day after day. We were close, yes. But we knew what had to come first. We had to win the war."

I allowed a half smile. "But the war is over now."

He stared at her for a long moment, hope in his eyes, unaware of my words. "When she wakes, thank her for me." He stepped away.

"Wait." He froze as I drew a note out. "You'll want this." Without his help, I would have been dead. All he asked in return was to find his sister. I owed him this much.

He shook his head after seeing the handwriting, unwilling to take it from me. "I don't understand. How do you have a letter from her?"

"You told me to find her."

He swallowed. "What does it say?"

"If you read it, you'll find out. It's not opened." Though the handwriting was definitely hers.

He shook his head, suddenly terrified. "What if it isn't good?"

"I can read it to you, if that would help." After a long moment, I tore the envelope open. "*Shandra. Thank you for this second chance. And thank you for finding my brother. I didn't know he was alive. Please tell him that I love him, and that I'm flying to NewAmerica now to be with him. And warn him,*

*will you, that York is coming too. He and I have an
announcement to make. Irene Boston.*"

"Curse the stars." He glanced at me with waves
of hope in his eyes. "She's coming here?"

"Yes."

"Is this even real?" He laughed, a noise that
morphed into panic. "I should go to her. Oh, she's
coming. How is she? Is she even well enough to
travel? Wait. How did she get the money?" He
paused suddenly, frowning. "Who's York?"

"I sent her the money." I shrugged. "I owed her.
And York—They were kind of a thing at the
palace."

"A thing." His brow furrowed as his scowl
deepened. "No one has a thing with my sister."

I hadn't thought about his reaction to York. "No.
Like, a good thing. They only kissed like—

"They kissed." His face flushed red.

I put my hand to my forehead. "They also
escaped Stroben's Palace together. And he saved
my life. Maybe give him a chance."

He shook his head. "I need to go deal with this."
His muscles loosened slightly. "And I need to see
my sister." There was a long silence before he
turned to go. "You'll be okay here, right? Like,
alone, waiting for when Nessa wakes up?"

"Boston, Irene is family. Go. I'll watch over
Nessa." I looked back at my friend. "If she wakes
up." She was, after all, unconscious.

"When." He walked out of the room. "When she
wakes up."

Nessa's finger twitched.

~

Leon stood in the viewing room of the World
Authority Association holding cells.
We were in a small room with prisoners lined up on
the other side of a window. "I don't see why this is
necessary."

The prison officer gave an annoyed shrug. "We
need an official statement. You have to identify
them. We can't press charges without this." I grit
my teeth, hating the governmental hoops we had to
jump through.

Leon frowned. "This is absurd. You know who
they are. I did not need to do this for Dallas, or the
scientist. They've both already been tried."

"Obviously. And they got ten years. I'm sure
they'll learn their lesson. But they're from
NewAmerica. These two are foreign. The rules are
different." The man wore an irritated frown. "Just
do it, and get out of here. Or, if you'd rather, we can
let them go free."

"Fine." Leon grit his teeth, his hand still
wrapped around mine. His fingers were shaking, but
his face was a mask of serenity. He looked directly
at Koren. "They can't see me?"

"Nope." The guard curled a lip, adjusting his
World Authority Association badge. "You can be
as much of a coward as you want."

I coughed, shocked at the man's rudeness, but
Leon was the one who spoke. "I won't point them
out unless you let Koren and Ceba look me in the

eye." As much as I wanted to just leave, I understood Leon's need for closure.

"You slave-brats are all the same, coming here. If you ask me, you're the pathetic ones. Now that there's guards around, you're finally building up the courage to face your demons."

Why did I trust the World Authority Association with this in the first place? All they did was give a slap on the wrist. "Leon, just point them out on this side of the glass, and let's leave. They never need to know we were here."

"I need them to know. I won't point them out unless you let me into that room. I don't care if you bring guards or not."

"What if they snap at you?" the guard gave a look of mock concern. "Or say mean things that hurt your slave-brat feelings?"

Leon stared at the captors. "Let me in that room."

The officers laughed, swinging the door wide open. Every prisoner was in chains, and wasn't allowed to move from their place. The guards, all seven, filed in first. Leon and I were instructed to speak as little as possible, to point at the slave catchers and leave fast. Though it seemed the main officer was expecting quite a show.

I was sick of people using Leon for their own amusement.

We stepped in. Koren and Leon locked gazes. "Ironic, that I'm the one in chains," Koren hissed. "When they belong to you."

A low-level security man drew his weapon. "There is no talking permitted."

But the main official waved a hand, allowing the communication to continue.

Leon took a step closer, his view falling to the ground. "Koren," he said without looking, pointing at him, then moving his gesture to the woman. "Ceba."

I shifted to leave, but Leon made no movement to go. He tried to speak, but only a choking sound escaped his lips. His face blushed, and shame masked his features.

I was burning to leave, but Leon wasn't willing to move. Time passed, one infinity after another.

After a long moment, he traced his scar, the white line where his tracker had been removed. His strength growing, he looked up, into Koren's eyes. "I'm not scared. Not of you. Not of Ceba. Not of Stroben. Not anymore." He turned on his heel, walking out of the room.

Allowing for only a half second, I turned to leave as well. It felt good, stepping away from the slavecatchers, standing as the victors. There were so many moments when Leon and I should have lost, died, yet here we were. We were triumphant. We were safe. We were free.

As I moved, I saw the expression on Koren's face morph, twisting to pure entertainment. "He should be afraid." Koren gave a Cheshire grin, his eyes flashing from the guards to me. "I do have this all under control. Tell him, Shandra, would you?"

A chill of fear flowed down my spine, but I willed it away. The World Authority Association had the power here, and they weren't about to let him walk free. The security guards had been less than charming, but they weren't incompetent. And they weren't that corrupt. They knew he was evil, and they wouldn't let him get away. He was going to live and die incarcerated. He would never see the outside of a prison again. He was bluffing. He had to be.

~

The room smelled of oil and sweat, and honest hard work. There was a new-model transport, painted red, sitting in the shop. The light from the windows struck it, reflecting around the room, catching the dust flecks in the air. In the corner, past broken machinery and replacement parts, there was a workbench. There, was Leon.

His hands were dirty. The rest of him was finally clean. He was sitting in his new shop, at the mechanical bench, surrounded by the clutter of his new life. The sound of the scratching of Leon's tool against the engine part played as a quiet music, soft, gentle, calm.

It was perfect for him. He was perfect, too, sitting, his back from me, on a simple wooden chair. The item he was working on was a part of a speeder engine. Apparently. His shoulders were relaxed, his back covered by a simple brown shirt. His head was tilted slightly to the left as he leaned forward, deeply involved in his work. He hadn't noticed that I'd stepped in.

"Leon."

He lifted his head, turning. "Shan." His face had a streak of grease across it, the front of his hair sloppy. He grabbed for a cloth to wipe off his hands. "What's up?"

I shrugged. I'd been working with Nessa and the World Authority Association. We were assisting the MiraCorp prisoners in their transitions back to the outside world. In his free time, Leon had been fixing transports.

"I was just in a meeting with the World Authority people. They were explaining why the MiraCorp prisoners couldn't be financially assisted in their transition. They were informing me that the creation of passports for those who wanted to leave NewAmerica.... Well, apparently, that just won't work." I lifted my hands in frustration. "It's like they're making my job harder on purpose."

He laughed. "Yes. Well. When Koren and Ceba got a grand total of six years, that's when I gave up on your Association. Turns out Stroben isn't the only one who is corrupt."

"Six. People get more than that for theft." I sighed, glancing over his bench. "What are you working on?"

He smiled. "It's a port clarity-enhancer for a RedBullet Skyline Cruiser."

I blinked.

"It's attached to windows in the port, and it removes rain and snow, any weather that decreases visibility. Only this one's wiper should be attached to the arm at this joint here." he pointed to the middle of the black arm-like structure. "But obviously, it's broken, and unattached. It's so mangled that I'm having trouble just taking the two halves apart."

"So it's like a broken windshield wiper from the antique cars?"

His expression morphed to comical horror. "Um. No. The window of the glass in a RedBullet is sharply acute, so the angles are so, so different. The old school cars have two wipers, coming up from the base. This wipes down from the top. It's much faster. It has to be, because It—" He took in my expression, my total lack of comprehension. "Yep. It's a broken windshield wiper."

I nodded. "I thought so."

"You're so annoying." He laughed, picking up the broken object, glancing to me for only the shortest of moments.

And we smiled at one another as I glanced at his pure presence—alive, happy, free.

Then he looked down, continuing with his work. For a time, there was no sound but the scratching. But then, he paused once more.

"You know," he said softly, as he tinkered, "I've been genuinely happy since I took over the shop. Working like this? Having friends, having choices, having my own path? I love it. It's like I have this light inside of me, some burning energy. I can't figure it out, but I feel like I was meant for it. I just—I'm so—I don't know. What even is this feeling?"

"This, Leon? This is freedom."

I would know. I was the Freedom Dreamer.

Acknowledgements

A thanks to everyone who picked up this book. Where would any novel be without the readers?

This story would never have been possible without my parents. Words fail me in my attempt to express your undying support.

Johnathan, thank you for ISBN input. Abigail, biggest fan, thank you. You know my stories better than I do. Samuel, thank you for your assistance with my plot synopsis.

The Malden Library Writer's Club also earned thanks. From your incredible disappointment in the name *Leon*, to your intense faith, you were amazing. To the member who shook my hand. I can only hope the story reaches others the way it touched your soul.

A thank you to Andrew, who suggested critical edits. To Laura, my cover specialist. To Thomas, who refused to read this story until it was worth reading. To Leanne. I can only hope Leon looks esthetic enough for you now.

To Emily, who told me to keep writing. Without you, Shandra would still be stuck in the desert.

To Cathy. The readers can see the sewers and desert now. To Susan, the first person who said she'd buy my book. No one in this novel is being 'killed to death' thanks to you.

To my English teacher. Your horror unit was my humble beginning.

To God, Author of the greatest story ever told.